THE
YELLOW
ROOM

JESS
VALLANCE

HOT
KEY
BOOKS

First published in Great Britain in 2016 by
HOT KEY BOOKS
80–81 Wimpole Street, London W1G 9RE
www.hotkeybooks.com

This is a work of fiction. Names, places, events and incidents are either the
products of the author's imagination or used fictitiously. Any resemblance
to actual persons, living or dead, or actual events is purely coincidental.

A CIP catalogue record for this book is available from the British Library.

ISBN: 978-1-4714-0581-5
also available as an ebook

This book is typeset in 10.5 Berling LT Std using Atomik ePublisher

Printed and bound by Clays Ltd, St Ives Plc

Hot Key Books is an imprint of Bonnier Publishing Fiction,
a Bonnier Publishing company
www.bonnierpublishingfiction.co.uk
www.bonnierpublishing.co.uk

For Mum

1

It's about half seven on Tuesday morning and it's freezing in my bedroom so I'm doing my usual trick of gathering all of my uniform together in one quick sweep, dragging it into bed with me and getting dressed completely under the duvet. It's only September and not even especially cold outside but there's something about our house, with its rattly old windows and too-big rooms, that means it's never really warm. There's also something about my mother and her refusal to put the heating on, which is probably a big part of the problem, but let's not get into that now. Anyway, I've just wriggled one arm into a shirt sleeve when the doorbell goes.

Jesus Christ. Sienna.

I know it will be my friend Sienna Rossi at the door because Sienna Rossi is the only person in the world who thinks seven-thirty-anything is an appropriate time for a social call. Although I suppose the truth is that Sienna doesn't really give much thought to appropriateness at all.

I scramble free of my duvet and stick my head out of my bedroom door to listen for signs of stirring or grumbling from Mum's room but all is quiet, so I'm guessing the bell hasn't woken her, which is definitely a good thing. I head downstairs, trying to button up my school shirt en route so as not to alarm the whole street when I open the front door.

I stand in the doorway. 'Sienna. Seriously. The doorbell? It's like seven a.m. People are sleeping.'

Sienna looks immaculate, as always. Her hair shines. Her eyes shine. She's a shiny kind of person. It's all her excess energy. Lights her up like a table lamp.

She pushes past me and into the hallway. 'Don't exaggerate, Anna. And I rang your phone and you didn't pick up so what am I supposed to do?'

'Not come over?'

Sienna heads down the hallway to the kitchen. 'Don't be such a miserable old arse. I wanted to get the bus with you. You like it when we get the bus together!' She opens the fridge and takes out a carton of milk. She pours herself a glass and downs it in one. 'Anyway,' she goes on, 'I don't know why you always make such a fuss. Your mum wouldn't wake up at this time in the morning if a swarm of piranhas came down the chimney and started eating her face.'

She has a point. Mum – or Dr Anita Castella, as other people call her – is a genetics researcher at the university and usually works till the early hours of the morning up in her attic study. She falls into bed around three or four in the morning, and it's an event if I see anything of her before midday.

'Although I don't know what piranhas would be doing in a chimney.' Sienna rinses her glass under the tap and rests it on the draining board. 'A piranha is a fish, isn't it? They'd swim up the toilet instead, right?'

I don't reply, but I doubt Sienna notices. Sienna doesn't concern herself with replies.

'Oh, guess what,' she says, sitting down at the kitchen table. 'I have the funniest story to tell you. You know that man my dad's friends with – the one who always comes round to clean out the gutters and all that? Brian? Well, last night he's over at my house and my dad says, "Thanks ever so much for your help, Brian." And Brian does this funny little look and he says, "You know, I've been meaning to ask for a while – why do you always call me Brian?" and my dad looks really freaked out suddenly and he says, "That's right, isn't it . . . Brian O'Neil?" and Brian says, "No, mate. Nearly but not quite. It's Neil O'Brian." Isn't that the funniest story you ever heard? Honestly, Anna, my dad's face was an absolute picture.'

'I need to finish getting dressed,' I tell her. I turn and head for the stairs. 'Make me some toast if you want to speed things up.'

I make some effort to make myself look presentable, sponging crusty tomato soup off my tie and pulling my hair back into a ponytail to disguise the fact it really could do with a wash. When I return to the kitchen, Sienna presents me with a plate of toast. She has elected to top it with coleslaw.

'It's nice,' she tells me when she sees my expression. 'I have it all the time. It's crunchy and tangy. And it's vegetables, so it's one of your five a day. No, wait – two! Carrot and cabbage, cabbage and carrot. Did you know there was this one American baseball player who always used to play with a cabbage leaf under his hat to keep him cool? Seriously. True story.'

3

I make myself eat a slice because there's no time for anything else. It's weird, so I go to throw the second slice away but Sienna takes it out of my hand and demolishes half of it with one bite.

'Why are you wearing odd shoes?' she asks, spraying crumbs everywhere.

I look down. 'I'm not. These are my normal shoes.'

Sienna frowns and peers more closely. 'Oh right, yeah. My mistake. I thought one was brown. But they're both black, so it's fine. Can we go now?' She's bobbing up and down on the balls of her feet like a sprinter waiting for the starter gun.

'Yes. Fine. Come on then.'

Halfway down the road to the bus stop we meet the postman, shuffling through a pile of letters, his bike resting against the wall. He has dreadlocks and tanned skin and I expect he does this job because he likes being outside.

Sienna stops walking. 'Excuse me, Monsieur le Postman, have you anything for number twenty-eight?' She leans forward and peers eagerly into his big red bag.

I take her hand and pull her towards the bus stop. 'Sienna, it's fine. I'll just pick it up when I get home. Don't mess with his system.'

'Why would you wait when he's right here with your post now? It's just sitting there, in that bag, with your name on it.'

I can't be bothered to argue. I stop and wait while the postman sighs and rummages through his bag.

'Twenty-eight . . . twenty-eight . . . Just this.' He hands Sienna an envelope and I take it from her before she gets carried away and rips it open. It's addressed to me, not Mum, which is surprising.

4

'See!' Sienna claps and throws her hands up towards the sky as if she has personally conjured the envelope into existence. 'I knew it!'

I look at the front of the envelope again, trying to work out if I recognise the curly handwriting. I decide I don't so I shove it into my bag and we continue on our way.

As soon as we take our seats on the bus – at the top, at the very front because Sienna likes to feel 'like we're flying a plane'– she's on at me again.

'Open it, then. Why would you not just open it? Someone has written a special message just for you and you're not even reading it. How can you stand it?'

I reluctantly pull the crumpled letter out of my bag. 'Christ on a bike, Sienna, how do you maintain this level of excitement about everything? You know it can only ever lead to disappointment. What exactly do you think it's going to be?'

'I don't know, do I? That's the whole point! There is nothing as exciting as a mystery!'

I rip the envelope open and tip the paper out. I notice it smells sort of like roses and soap. Sienna tries to take the letter from me but I snatch it back and turn away from her to read.

Dear Anna,

This is my fourth attempt at writing this letter. All the others are in balls in the bin. I've given up trying to come up with the right way of saying it so I'll just get to the point.

*My name is Edie Southwood. I've spent most of the
last eight years with James Roddick. We weren't
married but we did live together like husband and
wife, you know how people do these days. I don't
know if anyone will have told you what's happened,
but I suddenly thought that maybe no one has, and
that doesn't seem right to me so I wanted to make
sure you knew. I'm so sorry, Anna, but James died
last week. These last few days have been the worst
of my life. I feel as if the bottom has fallen out of
my world and most days I'm not sure whether
I can carry on at all. It's a loneliness I had
never imagined.*

*I move through each hour feeling like I've died myself.
Nobody speaks to me. Nobody looks at me. Sometimes
I wonder if I'm really here at all. Maybe I'm not.
Maybe I'm a ghost – one of those spirit beings who
can't quite accept they've gone. Are you reading this,
Anna? Are you there? I suppose if you are then I'm
really here too. This letter can be the test.*

*I was wondering, Anna, if you would meet me? At
this stage, I don't truly believe anything would make
things better but I do feel as if seeing you – what's
left of my wonderful James – might help in some
way. Perhaps you too will have some questions that I
could help answer. I also have something to give you.
Something James wanted you to have.*

I hope to hear from you soon, Anna.

Best wishes,
Edie Southwood

I read the letter through twice. I suppose I'm shocked. Not upset as such, but surprised, definitely. It certainly wasn't news I'd expected to get on my way to school this morning.

'What is it?' Sienna takes the letter from me and scans it. 'Well, this is weird. Who's this James character?'

I look out the window. An old lady is being pulled along by a dog twice the size of her.

'My dad.'

2

Sienna's hand flies up to her mouth and she scans over the letter again. Her eyebrows are halfway up her forehead. 'Oh, Anna,' she says shaking her head. Her voice is breathy and shocked. It's Sienna in classic drama mode.

'It's OK.' I take the letter back from her and push it into the envelope. 'It's not a big deal.' I rest my feet on the ledge in front of us and lean my head against the window. I'm tired. I don't want to talk about it.

'Oh, Anna,' she says again. 'It *is* a big deal. The most massive deal ever! I'm so sorry. And this seriously is the first you've heard about it? Was he very sick, do you know?'

I shake my head and draw a stick-man in the condensation on the glass. 'I dunno. But really, it's fine. We weren't exactly in touch.'

'Well, I know not recently, but still, your dad is your dad is your *dad*, you know?'

I shrug. 'Technically.'

My father moved out of our house when I was four. I have only vague memories of him – his gelled hair, the smell of coffee. His brown, shiny shoes. He never took his shoes off,

8

I remember that. He was always tap-tap-tapping along the wooden floor. Maybe he knew he wasn't staying long.

I'd got a few birthday cards from him in the early years, for my sixth and seventh birthdays, perhaps my eighth. I saved them all in their original envelopes in the drawer under my bed. I can't have treasured them that much though, because I didn't notice when they stopped coming and, in fact, I'd forgotten all about them until I was around eleven or twelve and was having a good clear out. It was only then, when I found them nestled between an old *Stars of WWF* sticker book and a *Lord of the Rings* jigsaw puzzle, that I noticed the handwriting – sloping to the right; round, looping Bs and Ps. Mum's handwriting.

I didn't feel angry. It was more of an 'oh, of course' type feeling, like when you finally work out that the reason the toaster isn't working is because it's turned off at the wall. And then I think I just felt stupid for ever believing they were from him at all. I calmly took the cards out of the drawer, folded each of them into four neat quarters and dropped them into my waste paper bin. I instantly, silently, wrote him off. I didn't have a father. But then, so what? I'd sort of already come to that conclusion and I was hardly the only one. I never confronted Mum about the forged cards. What would be the point?

'I know it's been a long time, but he was your *father*, Anna. Your flesh and blood.' Sienna really isn't the type to let a subject go.

I roll my eyes. It's hard not to find her annoying at times like these. I mean, credit where credit's due, she *is* genuinely caring, but sometimes I can do without her turning everything

9

into her own personal soap opera. I just want to be left alone to process my news on my own.

'Would you care if you found out your birth parents were dead?' It's easier to turn the conversation back on her, to take some of the pressure off me.

Sienna seems surprised by the question, even though it's an obvious comparison. Sienna was adopted when she was six months old by a lovely couple of theatre actors – Lorenzo and Constance Rossi. They adore Sienna and they're also absolutely loaded. The perfect combination.

She leans back in her seat and looks out of the window for a minute. At first I think I've pissed her off but then I realise she's just thinking. 'It's different though, I think,' she says after a while. 'Like, no, I wouldn't be that bothered. But then I have a dad. I have a mum. I don't need another set. That was your one and only dad. And now he's gone.'

'It's *fine*, Sienna. I don't care. I didn't even know him any more. He was just a random man living with some random woman in some house miles away from here. They're nothing to me. Either of them. I do not *care*.'

I'm annoyed with Sienna for making me say all this. By going in all heavy with the sympathy like that, she's made me go to the other extreme and now here I am making a big hoo-ha of the whole no-big-deal angle when really I would've liked five minutes to myself to work out just how much of a big deal it actually is.

Two stops and eight minutes later, George Shanklin joins us on the top deck of the bus. George, Sienna and I make up a sort of group, I suppose. I'm normally with one or the other of them, or more often than not, both. The three of us met in Year Nine when they both started at our school, Frederick Cross Academy. Some people – like me, for example – start at our school in Year Seven, but some others join later in Year Nine, when they move up from middle school. Sienna and George were already friends from middle school when they joined my tutor group, and they were so inseparable, the back-and-forth banter so constant, I'd asked if they were a couple. Sienna had been quite quick to correct me there.

'Oh, holy mother of god, NO. The only way Georgie could get someone like me would be if he bought me off the internet,' she told me that first day.

'Oh, behave yourself, love,' George responded. 'I could think of better ways to spend a fiver, thank you very much.'

They didn't waste any time being polite to me either. The first conversation I ever had with George went like this:

George: What's your name?
Me: Anna Roddick.
George: Ha! Are you a porn star or what?
Me: What?
George: Anne Erotic!
Me: No. Anna. Rod*dick*.
George: Oh.

George sits down in a seat behind us. 'All right, dickhead?' he says to Sienna. 'All right, Spanner?' He deliberately messes up my hair, but I bat his hand away.

'Don't.' I carry on looking out the window.

11

'What the matter with her?' he asks Sienna.

'She's had some bad news,' Sienna tells him gravely. I don't look at them. She slides the letter out of my hand and passes it to George.

He scans it, his chin resting on the back of my chair. 'Who's James, then?'

'Her *dad*,' Sienna hisses, as if I can't hear.

'Woah.' George looks at the letter again. 'Shit, man. So your dad is really *dead*? Shit.'

I don't move my head. I stay focused on the window. In the reflection I can see them mouthing words at each other. I can't tell exactly what they're saying but I can tell from George's exaggerated shrugs that they're trying to work out what they should say next.

'How did he die?' George asks.

'We don't *know*.' Sienna is still whispering.

'I'll Google it,' George says, taking his phone out of his pocket.

I turn to look at him. 'What? Why? The internet won't know. He wasn't a celebrity.'

'Yeah but if he was like, murdered or swallowed up by a sink hole or something, then it'll know about that. It'll be in some local newspaper or whatever.'

Sienna and I watch while George taps away at his phone and frowns at the screen.

'So,' I say eventually, 'was he murdered or swallowed up by a sink hole?'

George shakes his head sadly. 'Doesn't look like it. Nah. Nothing.'

'What did you put in?' Sienna asks.

12

'*James Roddick dead*. And *James Roddick died*.'

I start to giggle suddenly. I know it's not really funny but it's just those two looking so serious – it's created some kind of weird reaction in me.

'What?' George says. 'What's funny?'

'This,' I say, holding the letter up. 'This Edie woman. What a mentalist! "The bottom's fallen out of my world!"' I shake my head. 'And all that stuff about being a ghost – what's *that* about? Seriously, I mean, get a grip, right? Get. A. Grip.'

Then George starts laughing too. I think he's relieved. I've given him permission to make a joke out of it all. George is always most comfortable when he's allowed to make a joke out of a situation. 'The bottom's fallen out of my world!' he says in a ridiculous high-pitched voice. 'The WORLD'S fallen out of my BOTTOM!'

This sets Sienna off too. She resists it at first but after a minute or two we're all sitting there, just laughing and laughing and it's a relief after the tense start to the bus trip.

But then suddenly, I don't know where it's come from but I feel like I'm going to cry. I don't though. I just stop laughing abruptly, push the letter to the bottom of my bag and look out the window. I swallow hard. My jaw aches. The others stop laughing too and I can see them looking at me out of the corners of their eyes.

'You all right, Spanner?' George says tentatively.

'Yeah. Fine.'

3

At lunchtime, the three of us sit in the canteen and George tells us about his latest business venture. George is kind of a wheeler-dealer. He calls himself an entrepreneur but I think that could be overstating things a bit. He picks up stuff in bulk and flogs it at school for a small profit. His latest offering is little offensive badges, the small, pin kind that people decorate their bags with. Each badge is white with a slogan written across it in neat black letters.

George takes a paper bag full of them out of his rucksack and offers them to us like a bag of sweets. 'Here you go, lucky dip. I'm selling them for one-fifty but for you I'll do a special offer: a quid each.'

I put my hand in and pull out a badge. I turn it over and read the slogan.

your face disgusts me

'Oh lovely, thanks.' I pin the badge to my tie.

Sienna cracks up. 'Brilliant! I love it! My go my go my go.'

Sienna dips her hand into the bag. She takes out a badge

and turns it round to show us.

She falls about laughing all over again.

'I'm here all week.' George grins. 'One pound each, please.'

Sienna waves her hand dismissively. I raise one eyebrow. I don't think either of us has ever paid George for one of his products.

George wanders off to hawk his goods and Sienna and I amble outside to the basketball courts.

I hear a voice call from behind me. 'Hey there! Anna!' I recognise it straight away. Leon Jakes-Field.

Sienna looks behind us. 'It's him *again*? Just ignore him. You shouldn't encourage these people, Anna. You do realise he is quite likely to turn out to be a psychopath?'

'It's fine. He's not that bad, just boring. You go ahead and I'll get rid of him. I just have to say one nice thing to him and it'll keep him quiet for a week.'

Sienna rolls her eyes and shakes her head. 'You are such a soft touch, Anna Roddick. No wonder you get all these undesirables pestering you.'

I shrug and give her an apologetic smile just as Leon catches up with us.

'Anna has had a bereavement, Leon. Try not to be an idiot,' Sienna tells him before marching away into school.

This is the least helpful thing she could've said. It gives Leon a conversation point. Leon looks for any excuse to start a conversation with me.

15

Leon Jakes-Field is in our year and is the son of Rebecca Jakes-Field – better known as R.M. Jakes-Field, author of the internationally acclaimed Orion Glass fantasy books. This was basically the first thing Leon told me about himself, back when I had to sit next to him in Year Eight geography. Like most people, I had heard of R. M. Jakes-Field – her first three Orion Glass books were picked up by some hotshot Hollywood type and so she'd started popping up on everything from *Good Morning* to *Question Time*. Leon had been quick to tell me that he too was a writer. He'd carry around a Moleskine notebook and could be seen making a big show of taking it out and scribbling notes into it when inspiration struck.

He also ran a creative writing club after school that he managed to persuade me to go to once. It was totally awful. I spent half an hour listening to Leon read out some terrible short story he'd written about a scarecrow in a cornfield (a metaphor for detachment from society or something) and then sat at the back of the room while a bunch of Year Seven boys queued up to give Leon their Orion Glass books for him to take home and ask his mother to sign.

I managed to make my excuses and get out of Leon's creative writing classes pretty quickly and planned to generally distance myself from him. Leon, though, had other ideas and spent much of our early years at Frederick Cross trying to engage me in conversation, offering his advice on everything from my school work to my clothes and leaving little presents in my locker or my coat pockets. To this day, I'm not sure why Leon homed in on me but I'm pretty sure I shouldn't take it as a compliment. It was probably my own fault for being civil to him when we first met.

I managed to keep him at bay and then put him off altogether by Year Nine, basically by being gradually more horrible to him until he seemed to lose interest, but since we've been back at school for Year Eleven, he's been following me around again, trying to start conversations, giving me advice. Finding excuses to touch me.

Just as I feared, Leon latches on to Sienna's bereavement comment straight away. 'Anna? What's happened? Come. Come talk to me.'

'It's nothing, seriously,' I say as he leads me over to a quiet corner of the basketball court. He reaches up and pushes a strand of hair behind my ear. I have to resist the urge to jerk my head away from his touch.

'What's happened?' he says again, his face unnecessarily close to mine.

I really cannot be bothered with this. Leon doesn't care about me. All he cares about is getting an opportunity to put his sensitive and mature man-of-the-world act into practice.

'It's no big deal.'

He sets his face into his favourite expression – I guess it's meant to look caring and concerned mixed with worldly and wise but I think it just makes him look like he's wet himself. 'Talk to me, Anna.'

I give myself a silent pep-talk: come on, Anna, you can get through this. Just play the part for five minutes. Just five minutes, then you've done your bit for the next couple of days.

I make myself smile a sad smile, lips pressed together, eyes looking down at my shoes. 'It was my dad. I found out this morning.'

'Oh, *Anna*.' Leon's mask of concern is ramped up to breaking point. If his forehead gets any more creased, small animals will start to build nests in the crevices. He leans forward and pulls me into an awkward hug. The smell of his sickly sweet aftershave makes me want to gag. No doubt he'd tell me it's something very classy and expensive but to me it just smells like the air fresheners they use in public toilets.

He holds on to me for too long. I sincerely hope no one is watching.

I pull away and give him a brave smile but I don't say anything. I figure the less I say the quicker the conversation will reach its natural conclusion.

Leon reaches into the inside pocket of his jacket. 'I've got something here actually, something that might help . . .' He takes out his Moleskine notebook and flicks through the pages. 'Yes, here. Here it is.'

He clears his throat. Oh, Jesus, he's going to read me something he's written.

'*Grief*,' he says in a clear voice, '*sadness. These twin demons, they descend . . .*'

I stop listening immediately. I look across the playground to some Year Sevens playing football. One of them steals the ball from another and sprints off down the playground. I feel like a prisoner forced to watch free people go about their lives through the bars on my window. Dear god, please let this be over soon.

I keep my face set into the expression most likely to please

Leon – sad, but clearly enthralled by his genius. He's obviously approaching the pinnacle of his creative work because he pulls himself up tall and steps forward like a boy band doing a key change.

'*But now, only peace. Only quiet. I can. I will.*' Leon closes his book and looks at me carefully, forcing me to hold eye contact. '*I know.*' He finishes.

He's looking at me for a reaction but I'm not sure exactly what he's expecting. Is it normal to applaud a poem? I decide a few feeble claps are easier than thinking of something complimentary to say.

'Thanks. That was great. It really helped.'

Leon nods modestly. I look at my watch. Surely I've done enough now. Surely now it's OK to end this whole excruciating encounter.

'I've got to go, I'm afraid. I've got to talk to Miss Hayes about this thing . . .'

Leon nods again. 'Of course, of course. Life must go on. But, Anna –' he opens his satchel and for one awful second I think he's going to get out another embarrassing poem to read, but instead he takes out a blank notepad and passes it to me – 'Please. Have this. I want you to have a go at writing down your feelings. I know you're not good at expressing your emotions but sometimes things flow more easily with a pen in hand. Try some poetry. It doesn't have to be Wordsworth, but practise articulating what you're feeling. I can help you craft it into something more refined later.'

I look down at the notepad. I wonder if anyone has ever received a less appealing offer. 'OK. Thanks.'

Leon looks at me carefully, his hands in his pockets and his head slightly on one side. Then he reaches out and touches my cheek. It makes my skin prickle. 'I'll help you. I'll help you find the words. Don't worry.'

I pull my head away. I just can't bear him any longer. I mumble something about being late and then I'm striding quickly across the courts and heading towards the main school building. I don't look back but I imagine that if I did, I'd see Leon waving me off, like a father waving his child off on a train platform.

When I arrive in our tutor room for afternoon registration, Sienna comes over to me. 'There you are! Tell me you haven't been with Leon *all* this time?'

I don't say anything.

'Anna.' She stands opposite me with her hands on my shoulders. She looks me right in the face. 'Anna, listen to me. You must *not* encourage him. You're only making it worse.'

I sigh and flop down in a seat. 'I know, I know. It's just –'

Sienna cuts me off, which is good because I don't know what I was going to say anyway. There is no reason for me to be putting up with Leon like this. No reason I can tell her about anyway.

'I know you can't resist a hopeless case, but Leon is a clinger. If you so much as look at him for too long he'll assume that you are engaged to be married.'

I just laugh and wait for the subject to change.

George sits up from where he has been lying flat on his back across two desks, his hands behind his head.

'She's right, you know,' he chips in. 'That bloke's got stalker written all over him. I'd steer well clear if I were you.'

20

I take out my homework diary and pretend to be engrossed in flicking through to find something. I don't have anything to say. I know they're right. I know Leon is a nutter. A self-important, patronising nutter. I know the more I talk to him, the worse he gets. But I also know something that they don't.

I know that if I don't keep Leon Jakes-Field on side then things could get a hell of a lot more uncomfortable than the odd unwanted poetry reading.

4

At home, I'm surprised to find Mum sitting in the kitchen. At this time of day she's normally either in her study or at the university; she's never just sitting around idly in the kitchen drinking coffee and eating buttered crackers like she is now. My first thought is that this unusual behaviour must be in some way connected to the news of the dead dad. All day I have been thinking about whether or not I should tell her, but now it occurs to me that maybe she has already been told.

I fill the kettle with water and flick it on. 'Aren't you working?'

Mum blinks like she's only just realised I'm there. 'Waiting for a phone call. From the University of Prague.'

'About the festival?'

'It's not a festival, Anna. There won't be fire jugglers and stinking Portaloos. It's a conference.'

'The *conference* then,' I sigh. This is what happens every time I make an effort to show an interest in Mum's work. She cuts me down, treats me like an idiot.

She's in the middle of organising some educational event about something to do with proteins and genes and 'transcription'. Whatever that means. All I know is that it's a big deal – to Mum, anyway. It's 'career-making stuff, Anna'.

Mum nods. 'I'm waiting to find out if Professor Alexej Chovanec can key note.'

I have no idea who that is or what it means but the way Mum looks up at the clock then at the phone then back to the clock again tells me that she's nervous.

Mum is young, for a mum. Almost twenty years younger than Sienna's parents, for example. I know she's very successful, that her work is important – like, actual life and death stuff – but the truth is, I've never really understood exactly what she does. I don't know what she's trying to find out or what she spends all those hours reading about up in her study. In fact, everything I know about Mum's work I found out by reading her staff profile page on the university's website. Mum has never really cared to explain it to me, not properly. I have tried to ask, not for a while, but before. But Mum would quickly become frustrated if I asked too many questions or if I didn't grasp the significance of it all at once. She'd tell me that I just wasn't getting it, that I was 'oversimplifying' things. I irritated her.

I think perhaps she used to try to involve me. I remember she'd do science experiments with me at home – something to do with red food colouring and jars of hot water – and she'd buy me science kits to play with, but I don't think I was the protégée she hoped for. I remember when I was six, she bought me a real microscope for Christmas but when she was trying to show it to me, to get me excited about looking at scabs and ants on the little glass tile, I got bored and was more interested in the fluffy toy dog I'd been given by some

23

old aunt, making it a bed on the sofa and pretending to feed it mince pies. I guess after a few years of that sort of thing she gave up on me. I was just too stupid.

I think Mum finds me just as irritating now. She finds a lot about the world outside her work irritating. It seems frivolous to her, I suppose. Once when I was little, we were about to leave for school when I pointed out that I had my jumper on inside out. Mum sighed an exasperated sigh – 'Take it off and put it on the right way them!' – as if wanting to be properly dressed was somehow silly and childish. Mum certainly doesn't concern herself with such trivial matters. She always just wears the first thing that comes to hand – huge old-man's shirts; Bermuda shorts in the winter. Kilts. When I was younger, I'd thought perhaps I *was* silly and frivolous. Why was I so concerned with things that didn't matter? Did I have a faulty, simple brain? But as I've got older, I've realised that there's nothing silly about wanting to wash my clothes every now and then or choosing to eat a proper meal at a sensible time rather than having a plate of raisins and cheeseburger at 10 p.m.

The phone rings and Mum jumps up like her stool is electrified.

'Hello? Yes, speaking. Yes, thanks for getting back to me.' She takes the handset and disappears into the lounge.

A couple of minutes later she returns. She's chewing on her lip. She drops the phone back into its cradle. Then she stands and stares into the middle distance, her hands on her hips.

'So . . . is he coming?' I ask.

Mum shakes her head. 'I don't know . . . maybe. They can't tell me yet.' She sighs. 'He has to come. He *has* to come.'

24

Then she turns and leaves the kitchen and I hear her make her way up the stairs to her study.

I'm still not sure if I need to bring up the issue of the letter from the Edie Southwood woman at all – Mum and I haven't spoken of Dad for years and years so I don't see why he needs to become a topic of conversation just because he's dead. But either way, I decide that today is definitely not the day. The more I think about it, the more I can't really imagine how the conversation would go. The exchange we just had – Mum distracted, on her way somewhere; me slightly on edge, not really sure what we're talking about anyway – is about as good as interactions get in our house these days. Though it's a hundred times better than how things used to be. A couple of years ago, Mum and I could barely be in the same room without things kicking off. She'd usually start it by doing something ridiculous – letting the bath overflow, leaving the back door open all night so a fox got in and ate the sandwiches I'd made for my lunch, putting red socks in with my white school shirts – and so I'd ask her to please not be so totally thoughtless and annoying. Then she'd say something mean about me being pedantic and nagging her and then before you know it, we're having a full-blown row. I don't know what's changed in the last year or so, but this doesn't happen as much any more.

Personally, I think it's Mum. I guess whatever she's working on isn't as hard-core as the project she used to be doing, and that leaves more time for real-world concerns like shutting doors and turning taps off. But maybe she'd say it's me. Maybe she'd say I'm less annoying now I'm a bit older. Or maybe she's just given up on me. Maybe she doesn't care enough to be annoyed with me any more. I'm just a person who inhabits the same space as her, not worth getting worked up about.

Either way, Mum gets on with her life and I get on with mine and I can't really imagine how a big heart-to-heart conversation about dads and death and the past would go. I can't imagine Mum having any sympathy for Edie Southwood and her grief and loneliness and her weird ghost complex. Mum doesn't really do sympathy.

I go to my room and read the internet for a while. Then I come back downstairs and make myself a cheese sandwich and a mug of hot orange squash and watch telly on the sofa under a blanket. I'm watching some fly-on-the-wall programme where a camera crew follows these two paramedics around as they try to pick up the pieces after skateboarding falls and bonfire accidents and heart attacks. It's mostly quite pointless and gross but there's this one bit where an old lady's husband dies and in the interview afterwards she says they'd been together sixty-four years and now she just can't get used to being without him and, even though he's been dead two weeks, every morning she accidentally takes two mugs out of the cupboard for morning tea instead of one. It's totally heartbreaking. I find myself sitting there with tears pouring down my face and dripping off my chin into my cheese sandwich. And then I find myself thinking of Edie. Does she still get two mugs out in the morning?

I realise then that I haven't even seriously thought about Edie's request to see me. I'd just sort of brushed it aside – 'No thanks' – like how you do when someone tries to do a survey on you in the street. But now here I am, sitting here feeling sad that I can't do anything to help this poor old widow woman on the telly and it occurs to me that maybe I should at least consider doing something for the poor widow woman who's actually asked for my help.

5

The following Saturday, Sienna, George and I spend the day at George's house. George's offensive badge enterprise really took off this week and he's completely sold out of stock, so today he's summoned us to help him create more.

'It's all very well buying cheap and selling for a profit,' he tells us as he boots up the laptop he and his older brother Archie share in the dining room, 'but you're always going to be limited that way, aren't you? I don't want to be a middle man all my life. I don't want to be relying on suppliers. I got to be making my own gear, you know?'

'Do you know how to do that, then?' I ask.

George looks insulted that I even had to ask. 'Course, mate. Course. It's just badges, innit. Look – designs are done. Just got to print 'em, cut 'em, stamp 'em. Bish-bash-bosh, job done.'

'Don't you need a machine or something?'

George opens a door in the dresser and pulls out a box. '*Voilà*.'

'How much did that cost you?'

'Hundred and fifty.'

'A hundred and fifty POUNDS?' Sienna and I go over now too and the three of us stand there looking down at the blue box.

'Yeah, but it came with enough kit for six hundred badges. Sell six hundred for one-fifty each, that's nine hundred quid. A phenomenal seven hundred and fifty pound profit. Impressive, *oui?*'

I nod but Sienna stands with her hands on her hips, peering at George over the top of her dad's reading glasses, which she has decided to wear even though they make her feel sick, on account of the fact she thinks they make her look 'bookish and erudite'. 'George Patrick Shanklin, you are never going to sell six hundred badges.'

'My middle name's not Patrick,' George points out.

Sienna shrugs. 'You don't have a middle name.'

'Exactly.'

'Exactly. How am I supposed to middle-name you if you don't have a middle name?'

George decides not to argue with that.

'Look, I can easy sell six hundred. You know how many I sold this week? One hundred. I can *easy* do that six more times.'

I scrunch my nose up. 'But nearly everyone in the year has one already, right? Isn't that going to make it hard to offload another six hundred?'

George puts his head on one side, thinking for a moment. 'You make an interesting point, Anna. You think the market is saturated. A fair comment. BUT –' He heaves the box up to the dining table. 'Number one: school is not my only market, and number two: this is a long-term project. I'm in no rush.

29

Badges keep, don't they? They aren't going to go off. They don't cost me money to store. I can sell these things in my own sweet time.'

Sienna rolls her eyes and flops down on the sofa but doesn't have anything to come back with. 'So why exactly do you need us?'

'Dude, we got six hundred paper discs to cut out.' He slides a pair of scissors across the floor to her, ignoring her protests.

It's a sunny September day but George won't let us work in the garden because he's worried the wind will play havoc with our handiwork, so we sit on the sofa by the open window and listen to the kids play outside.

George lives in Kings, a new estate on the east side of town. All the houses are kind of ugly up here but there's something I really like about it. All the roads are arranged around little patches of green where kids ride bikes and play football and there are loads of dogs darting about that seem to belong to everyone rather than no one. I like George's family a lot. I think everyone likes the Shanklins a lot. There is a lot of them to like. George has an older brother, Archie, who's eighteen and is almost never without his saxophone, and two little sisters – six-year-old twins Daisy and Mae. They're totally adorable. George's mum and dad, Sally and Pete, run a cake shop by the pier and every Saturday at the end of trading they bring home any cream cakes that are left over and lay them out along the kitchen table. Then they just leave the back door open and all the local kids just drop in and help themselves. Sometimes they'll just sit down at the table and stay for a while and chat to Sally and Pete.

Pete is a big man with tattoos down both his arms. He's a total gentle giant type, and kind of like a huge human Venus flytrap – if any one of his kids comes within a three-foot radius of him he can't help but pull them into a bear hug. Often we'll just be sitting in the lounge watching TV or whatever and he'll walk past, ruffle George's hair and say, 'Love ya, boy,' absent-mindedly and George will barely even look up. It's all so completely far away from how things are in my own silent, tense house that I find it hard to believe we're part of the same species.

When we've cut out a hundred and thirty paper discs all of us have sore red patches on our fingers. Sienna throws her scissors dramatically down onto the floor. 'Enough! I've had enough!'

I stretch my arms up above my head and look down at my own little pile.

hair like a dog

kiss my elbows

piano teeth

George sighs and looks forlornly at the pile of discs still waiting to be cut out, but I guess he realises he's already pushed his luck. 'I think the cakes will be here by now anyway.'

He's right. Pete is unloading bags of doughnuts, and Daisy, Mae and a little boy I don't recognise have already taken their seats at the table. Once I asked George why his parents always have such a surplus of stock – 'Wouldn't it be better if they just didn't order so much?' – but George just shrugged, and I have a pretty good idea that the Shanklins wouldn't change the Saturday afternoon cake-fest for anything.

'Anna, love,' Sally says as I go in and take my seat at the table next to Mae, 'George told me about your dad. I'm ever so sorry.'

I see George and Sienna exchange a glance – nervous, awkward. Neither of them has mentioned my dad nor Edie's letter since my weird laughing/not laughing episode on the bus. I guess I'd thought they just weren't interested but seeing this little look between them now I can see they were deliberately avoiding the issue. They've actually been trying to be sensitive about it. I'm kind of touched.

'It's OK,' I say with a shrug. 'I hadn't seen him for ages. I haven't really thought about it much.'

'That letter sounded a bit odd though, from that woman? Georgie was telling me about it. I mean, she didn't sound quite well to me – all that talk about being a spirit. I hope she gets some help.'

I don't say anything. I didn't think the letter was that weird, was it? She was just upset, right? Sally looks at me for a minute, then gives my shoulder a squeeze and passes me a cream slice.

When we've had a cake each, George tells us it's time to get back to the production line, but I've had enough for one day. It's not just the scissors I want to get away from. I just want to be on my own for a while. I tell George it's time for me to go.

He looks surprised. 'Why, what's up?'

'Nothing. Just got to get home.'

32

He frowns at me for a moment, his head on one side. 'Is it to do with your dad and that crazy's letter again? Man! I knew I shouldn't have told Mum. She always has to say something.'

I shake my head. 'Nah. Nothing like that. Just got stuff to do, you know. See you later.'

I collect my things and head out the door before anyone can ask any more questions, leaving George and Sienna looking at each other in that way they have been lately, like they think I'm not quite right.

The truth is, what Sally said has made me feel kind of weird and uncomfortable. I don't really understand why. I guess it's like this Edie woman is going through a totally awful, rough time and she wrote all this heartfelt stuff in her letter and now here we are calling her a crazy. I guess what I'm feeling is guilt. Which is weird because I hardly think I owe the woman anything.

I think about Edie all the way home. I just can't get her out of my head. I think it's all the unknowns – what does she look like? What was her life like with James? What's it like now?

Why do I care so much?

6

When I get home that evening I head straight to my bedroom. I notice the smell in there straight away – that sickly vanilla-sweet air freshener smell.

Leon's aftershave.

I stand in the middle of my room, looking around me as if he might be there somewhere, hiding in a cupboard, watching me. But then after a few moments I'm not sure if I can smell it at all any more. Did I just imagine it?

I go downstairs to the front door and take a few deep breaths of fresh air. Then I go back into my room. It hits me again immediately. I'm not imagining it. It definitely smells of him. Then I notice the book on the desk. I pick it up and read the title.

Celtic Meditative Poetry

A yellow piece of paper is tucked just inside. I tug it out.

I thought this might help with your grief.

Poetry is a tonic for the soul.

L x

I look around me again. Maybe he didn't actually deliver the book here himself. Maybe his rancid aftershave is so strong that the book has absorbed the smell and is now emitting fumes everywhere it goes, like a sickly chemical weapon. Maybe it came in the post, or maybe he just dropped it on the door-step and Mum brought it up or something.

I'm about to head upstairs to ask her when my phone beeps. It's from Leon, a picture message. I open it and see he's sent me a photo of himself. He's standing in my room, leaning casually against the window sill. He's taking the photo with one hand, and in the other he's holding a book at chest-height, showing it to the camera. I zoom in to look more closely at the cover and I see it's my copy of *To Kill a Mockingbird*. Although technically speaking it's a school copy that I should've returned two years ago. Under the photo he's written:

Book swap! Let's chat soon. xx

I go over to my window sill, to the spot where he was leaning in the photo, and give it a vigorous wipe down with the towel that's hanging over my radiator. Then I take my phone and start to compose a reply to his text:

Leon, you can't just come into

I delete it and start again.

Why did you take my book

I delete this one too, then I throw my phone down on my bed and charge up the stairs to Mum's study. I don't bother to knock.

'Did a boy come here? Leon?' I demand. 'Did you let him in my room?'

Mum is hunched over her laptop, typing fast. She doesn't stop at first. She waits till she gets to the end of her sentence. Then she slowly turns her chair around to look at me.

'Excuse me?'

'Did a boy come to the house and did you let him in my room?'

She turns back around to her computer and stares at the screen.

'I've told you before about knocking. You've completely ambushed my train of thought.'

I want to shout but I also want her to answer so I make myself pause and calm my voice. 'Yes. Sorry. I'm sorry but –'

'Yes, there was a boy. He said you'd borrowed something of his and he wanted to pick it up.'

'Well, that was a lie.'

Mum doesn't reply.

'So you let him in my room?'

She looks at me again. I can see she is getting impatient. 'I'm not going to spend half an hour rooting through all of your junk, am I? He said he knew what he was looking for.'

I really want to lose it with Mum, to tell her that I should be able to count on my own mother not to let creepy, waistcoated

36

stalkers into my bedroom, but I need to stay focused on my goal here. My goal is to make sure that Mum knows not to let Leon in again.

I breathe out slowly. 'In future, I'd really prefer it if you didn't let people in my room when I'm not here. Please just ask them to come back later.'

Mum does a little shake of her head and rolls her eyes. 'Fine. Fine. When that mockney red-head comes around next time I'll shut the door in his face.'

Mum has known George for two years. She knows his name. She just chooses not to use it to make it clear to me how insignificant she finds all areas of my life.

My teeth are gritted. 'My friends are fine, *obviously*. George and Sienna are fine. Why do you have to be so difficult? It's just a simple request.'

Silence. Mum's acting like I'm not here at all now. It's extremely annoying.

'What I don't get,' I go on, 'is why you spend so much time locked up here supposedly trying to find out ways to help people – people you'll never even meet – but when your own daughter asks you for one simple favour you have to make a massive deal out of it. I guess it's because there's no glory in doing something for your own child, is there? No one's going to be giving out fancy science medals for that. And do you know why that is? It's because it's expected. You are expected to help your own family!'

I shout this last bit, but Mum doesn't shout back. Instead, she does something I hate even more – something she often does when I lose my temper with her – she laughs. A cold, hollow laugh. She turns to look at me. 'If you find living here so unsatisfactory you're more than welcome to move out. I certainly won't stand in your way. Pleasant though your company is.'

I slam the door hard and thunder back down the stairs. I sit on my bed and look at the photo of Leon on my phone. His fat, pink face. His lank greasy hair, parted at the side. That sinister sneering smile. My hand is shaking. I want to scream.

I badly want to send an aggressive text – to tell him I hate him, that he's repulsive. To tell him to never come near me again. I even type out the message, just for the sake of catharsis, but I know I can never send it. He would never let me get away with that.

In the end I decide not to reply at all, to act as if the whole bedroom intrusion never happened. But then, at about half past ten, another message comes through. It's another picture message. It's of my book, open and face down, resting on his chest – his naked chest.

Enjoying the book!

I know I have to reply. He won't stand for being ignored. That'll only make him seek me out at school, demand to know if something's wrong, if I want to 'talk about it'. I send a short message:

Great! Thanks for mine!

A few seconds later, he replies.

Sweet dreams, Anna xxxx

I just can't bring myself to reply to that. I put my phone in the drawer next to the bed and shut it hard, as if to prevent Leon's photo from climbing out in the night and accosting me. I badly want to ring Sienna or George and tell them about the whole disturbing episode, but I can't. I have thought about telling them everything about Leon – Sienna particularly would be great to have on side as she hates Leon as much as I do – but I can't risk it. I'm alone on this one. Totally alone.

And then it happens so quickly that it's sort of automatic:

I open the drawer next to my bed. I take out my phone, I take out Edie's letter, and I call her number.

7

It's fifteen hours since I called Edie and I'm sitting in The Last Drop, an old-fashioned cafe on the seafront, nervously fiddling with the sugar sachets in a bowl in front of me and looking at the door every thirty seconds.

When I rang Edie's phone last night she didn't answer, so I left a voicemail. I never leave voicemails as a general rule, but then I never call people I've never met before and arrange to meet for tea, so this whole thing is new for me.

I was quite transactional about it all in my message. I'm always awkward talking to a machine so I didn't say anything about my dad dying or sorry about her loss or anything like that. All I said was that I'd be willing to meet her and gave her directions to The Last Drop.

As soon as I'd hung up I felt bad, worried that I'd sounded rude or odd, wishing I'd said something a bit more sensitive, or at least acknowledged her 'situation'. I also worried that I wouldn't hear back from her so would have no way of knowing whether to go ahead and turn up at The Last Drop or not. But half an hour after my call, I got a text.

So pleased to hear from you. I'll be there. Edie.

So here I am, sitting and waiting and wishing we had actually spoken last night, that I'd had the chance to hear her voice to get a bit of an idea of her – her personality, her emotional state. As it is, I honestly don't know what to expect. She could be old, she could be young. She could be bright and breezy. She could be a snivelling wreck. She could be painfully shy and quiet. This is the one I'm dreading the most, even more than the crying-mess option. If she doesn't have a word to say for herself I'm not sure I'll be able to carry the conversation at all and I don't know how long I'll have to stay before I can make my excuses.

I look around me. I haven't been in The Last Drop for ages. It's not a popular hang-out spot for people from school, which is exactly why I've chosen it. It's about as basic as cafes get. Your traditional greasy spoon. Plastic tables with plastic table cloths on top of them and plastic chairs under them. Plastic cutlery too if you get here after ten at night because Martina, the woman who owns it, always thinks that if she leaves metal forks lying around the place, some drunken gang will rock up and start stabbing each other with them.

A while ago I briefly worked at The Last Drop and Martina terrified me. She's an enormous Estonian woman with wild eyebrows, hair in a single plait down her back and a voice like a trombone.

On a Sunday morning, I'd be in charge of cooking fry-ups for pensioners, who usually came in on their own and had a tendency to hang around for ages after they'd eaten, making a

41

cup of tea last an hour or more. Martina was having a crackdown on this unacceptable behaviour when I arrived as she'd decided that the key to increased profits was increased speed – 'We get them in, we feed their greedy faces, we throw them out. You understand me?' Sometimes I would have just laid the strips of bacon in the pan when she would appear behind me and loom over my shoulder.

'Is ready now,' she'd say, nodding her huge eyebrows towards the pan.

'I only just put it on.'

'Is ready now. Is fine. Serve.'

And I'd be forced to take some bemused pensioner a plate of lukewarm floppy bacon, unconvincingly disguised with a gallon of ketchup. If said pensioner then lingered too long over their substandard breakfast, Martina would swoop down on them and whip the half-empty plate from their hands. 'Is finished,' she'd tell them, ignoring any objections. 'Is gone.'

I eye Martina nervously now, half afraid that she'll throw me out before Edie has a chance to turn up. Luckily though, she seems preoccupied by some kind of pudding crisis. She's leaning into the kitchen with two rejected bowls of ice cream, shouting, 'Is no good! Is melted! Is lumpy like cat vomit. Make again!'

It's a stormy day, the rain lashing against the window and the seafront wind buffeting the signs outside so much that Martina is forced go and wrestle with them, the metal sheets billowing like sales.

'Wind,' she mutters as she comes back inside. 'Always wind in this town. Is problematic for me.'

42

Every time a person comes in the door I sit up a little straighter just in case it's Edie and they come over to my table. Every new person I think could be her – even when it's someone totally inappropriate like an ancient granny with a headscarf. Or a man.

I'm starting to drive myself crazy so I read a newspaper, just to keep my eyes off the door. In the end I don't even hear her come in. I just look up and there she is, in the middle of the room and she's looking at me and I'm looking at her and for some reason I just know at once it's her.

This is definitely Edie.

8

She has lots and lots of curly hair piled on top of her head with a few rain-soaked tendrils hanging around her face. She seems to be wearing an awful lot of clothing – layers and layers of skirts and frilly blouses – but all over the top of some chunky workman-type boots. She's carrying a big black-and-white spotted umbrella.

'Anna?'

I nod once, but don't say anything. I don't know what to say. I stand up because it seems rude to stay seated.

She comes over to me and looks into my eyes. 'Anna,' she says again. I think she's going to hug me but she just reaches out and shakes my hand – only she takes my left hand in her right, so it's more like holding hands. It's strange. I want it to stop.

'Thank you so much for coming,' she says.

'That's OK.'

She has an accent. I think it's from the West Country. It's sort of farmer-ish, anyway.

'Have you come far?' I ask.

'London,' she says, shaking off her umbrella.

44

Oh. Maybe I'm wrong about the accent. Or maybe she just moved. I suppose that's possible.

Martina approaches our table. 'I get you something.'

Edie picks up the menu. 'Uh, yes . . .'

'Tea, coffee, hot chocolate,' Martina prompts. Evidently cutting down on unnecessary menu-browsing time is the latest efficiency initiative.

'Just a tea, please.'

Martina nods once and turns to me. 'And you?'

'Uh, no, I'm fine, thanks.' I gesture to the mug already in front of me.

Martina peers down at it. 'Is finished,' she says. 'Another.'

I have a feeling this isn't a question, so I just nod.

Martina strides off towards the kitchen, shouting instructions to the mousey-looking teenage girl who must be my replacement.

'Blimey O'Reilly,' Edie says, leaning forward and giving me a nervous smile. 'That one's a bit fierce, isn't she?'

I grin and nod. 'Yeah. She really is.'

We wait for Martina to bring our drinks and Edie chats away about the weather and the sea and the cafe and her train journey down and I realise that I needn't have worried about awkward silences. Still, though, I get the feeling we're sort of warming up – soon this chatter will move onto more serious matters. The reason for our meeting.

I'm right.

There's a pause while Edie sips her tea and looks around. I can sense the change in her demeanour. It's coming.

'Had you heard, before my letter? About your dad?'

I shake my head. Edie nods a grim nod. 'I had a feeling that might be the case. I was thinking, surely she'll already know, won't she? And then the more I was thinking, I wasn't sure *who* would tell you, and then I started to feel bad that you didn't know at all and I felt a kind of responsibility, you know? And so I decided to write to you but it was hard to write it down because I didn't know what the right thing to say was, and then I thought I'd rather talk to you face to face but then I thought, well I need to tell you *why*, I can't just summon you with no reason . . . so anyway. I did my best. I'm sorry if I was cack-handed about it. Did I upset you?'

I shake my head again but then I realise I should probably say some actual words before Edie starts to think I'm a mute. 'It was fine. I was a bit shocked but I hadn't seen my dad for years and years anyway, so . . .'

I'm not sure how to finish the sentence. It seems a bit insensitive to say 'I wasn't that bothered', when Edie's already told me in her letter that the bottom fell out of her world or the world fell out of her bottom or whatever it was.

Edie nods but doesn't ask another question so I say, 'How did it . . . how did he . . .?'

I'm worried that it's not OK to ask this and that Edie might start crying but she doesn't. She just looks into her cup and says, 'Stroke. He was young, of course, for all that, but he was highly strung. His work, it meant a lot to him.'

'What work was it?' I realise it's ridiculous that I don't even know what his job was. I remember he used to go to work in smart clothes. He had a briefcase. But then, didn't everyone?

'Advertising,' Edie says. 'Business development for an ad

company. Schmoozing clients, keeping the money coming in. A lot of responsibility.'

I nod. That figures, I think. Advertising. Sales. Making empty promises.

'I wasn't there.' Edie says this quickly. It's a confession.

I look up. 'When he died? He was . . . at work?'

Edie shakes her head. 'He was at home. But I wasn't. I was at a hotel . . . a B and B. We'd had a row . . . silly. I'd been there a few days, waiting for him to ask me to come home – he always did in the end. When I got the phone call, it was from our home number. I thought it was him, of course. Calling to say sorry, ask me back. But it was his colleague. He didn't want to tell me the news on the phone, but I knew straight away he was being strange. He was being nice! He was horrible usually. Marcus, his name was. James's assistant. Really full of himself. But on the phone he sounded nervous. That's how I knew something was wrong.'

Edie looks away towards the window like she's lost in her thoughts. She seems to forget I'm there for a minute.

I want to ask more questions – what happened next, was he already dead or in hospital at this point? What about the funeral? Did anyone go? They all seem inappropriate though. The idea of asking them makes me feel like a tabloid journalist looking for a scoop. I realise, of course, that the best thing to do is to not focus on the death aspect at all. Edie would probably much prefer to talk about the alive bit instead.

'What was he like, my dad?'

Edie smiles then, a soppy kind of smile. And then she closes her eyes for a second, like she's gathering her thoughts.

'He was . . . he was a man of extremes.' She does a little sigh. 'He'd get excited about things – ideas, his work, plans we'd make for the future. Then he'd be all go, rushing around the place. Talking and talking. But if he got a set-back, he'd get down. He'd go quiet, for days. Brooding. Ignoring me completely. Nothing would snap him out of it. Nothing would make him talk to me. Nothing I could do, anyway. But he *would* always snap out of it eventually. And then he'd be back to his old self, all apologies and flowers.'

I nod but don't say anything. Personally I think he sounds like a bit of a dick.

I suppose Edie notices that I don't seem impressed so far because she seems in a hurry to reassure me. 'Of course, everyone's got their ways. I'm no saint myself. But I can tell you for sure that life with James is – was – always interesting. He was a good partner. He looked after me. I could rely on him. He felt a responsibility to me and it was important to him that he honoured those responsibilities.'

I feel my eyebrows twitch a little bit. I'm not sure how she can sit here and talk about responsibilities knowing that he just ditched me and Mum eleven years ago and didn't even bother to ring. I guess Edie notices my look because she seems to change her tone. She sits up and drops the dreamy expression.

'Anyway. Anyway. He's . . . now he's gone. That was then. This is now. So now I've got to find a way to . . . to start again.' She does a smile but it drops away quickly. She takes a sip of her tea.

Edie seems less chatty suddenly. I know I've not been that friendly so far. I wonder if she's regretting this meeting. I'm pretty sure I am.

'Oh,' she says, suddenly reaching for her bag. 'The thing. A thing, for you.'

She opens her bag and takes out a red velvet box. She pushes it across the table to me.

I look at it uncertainly. 'So . . . he left this . . . for me?'

Edie does a gesture that is somewhere between a shrug and a nod. When I keep looking at her she nods again, more firmly this time. 'Uh huh, yes. For you.'

I open the box and take out a thin silver chain with a cross pendant on it.

I look at Edie. 'A necklace?'

I can see it's a necklace but I suppose I was hoping she'd introduce the item to me – explain where my dad got it, why it was important, why he wanted me to have it. That kind of thing.

She doesn't though. She just nods once. 'A necklace, yes. A necklace.'

'Do you know where he got it?'

Edie frowns slightly and picks up the box, checking the bottom of it for clues. 'I can't remember exactly . . . I think it was a present. From a friend, maybe . . . I can't remember.'

'Oh. Right. OK. Thanks.' I drop the necklace back onto its cushion, snap the box shut and slip it into my pocket. 'Thanks,' I say again. 'For bringing it.'

I feel strangely deflated about my inheritance. I hadn't expected anything. I hadn't wanted anything. I certainly wasn't after anything of any monetary value. I just suppose I'd hoped for something with a story. A clue into my father's life, or at least a reason why he'd chosen the item for me. It seems a weird thing to pick out. I wouldn't have been at all surprised if he hadn't left me anything. I would've expected that, in fact. But giving me this one item without explanation or reason feels odd. I wonder if there's something Edie's not telling me. Maybe he didn't leave it to me at all. Maybe she's just told me that to make me feel better, to make me feel like he'd thought of me when in actual fact he'd completely forgotten I'd ever existed.

I can't think of anything else we can talk about after this. I suppose I could ask more questions but I suddenly realise I don't really want to hear about Edie's life with my dad. I thought it might be interesting, but it's not. When she talks about him, I just find it annoying. It's too frustrating to not be able to get any answers.

I wonder why I came. It wasn't really to see what she had to give me – I could've asked her to post it and I wasn't that bothered about it anyway. I suppose really it was out of guilt. It was because I had the power to do something to make someone who was feeling really bad feel a bit better, and so not doing anything would be really awful and selfish. But now we're here I really doubt I am doing anything to make Edie feel better so the whole thing feels like a waste of time. I find my eyes wandering towards the door. I wonder whether if I just got up to go to the loo, I could just slip out and . . .

The door opens.

Oh, god. It's Leon.

9

My instinct is to look down – that silly childish idea that if I'm not looking at him, he can't see me. It doesn't work, of course.

'Ah! Anna!' he calls and makes his way over. Leon is not the type of boy to be put off by the fact I clearly already have company.

'Christ,' I say under my breath.

Edie gives me a questioning look but there's no time to explain because Leon is already at our table. He pulls a chair over from a neighbouring table and sits down, one foot resting confidently on the opposite knee.

'Hello there,' he says brightly. 'What a delightful surprise.'

'Hi,' I say, looking pointedly towards Edie. It feels a bit too risky to just outright tell Leon to leave or that now isn't a good time – being made to look a fool really winds him up – but I'm hoping that he'll take the hint and twig that I'm busy.

He doesn't.

'Hi there!' he says again, this time offering Edie his hand. 'I'm Leon Jakes-Field.'

Leon always includes his surname any time he introduces himself. He'd never just say 'I'm Leon' because how would people make the connection to his famous mother that way? How would they ever realise that he has literary genius in his blood?

Edie looks down at his hand, but instead of shaking it, she turns away from him, takes a sharp intake of breath, buries her face in her hands and starts to sob loudly.

Leon and I stare at her for a second, blinking stupidly. Leon's hand is still outstretched, hovering in mid-air. He withdraws it and lets it fall onto the table. He looks at me but I just shrug.

I reach out and rub Edie's upper arm awkwardly. 'Uh . . . don't cry,' I say lamely.

'Is she OK?' Leon hisses, as if Edie isn't sitting right there next to us.

I give him another shrug, this one with a bit of a wince thrown in for good measure, and say, 'It's a bad time for her.'

I'm quite deliberate with my tone and facial expressions here. The impression I'm going for is apologetic, embarrassed. I'm trying to convey a message to Leon that says, 'Obviously I'd really rather you stayed but I should probably deal with this mess. *So* sorry.' This way, hopefully, I'll get him to leave without pissing him off too much.

It seems to work. Leon stands up awkwardly, wiping his hands on his jeans as if he's worried he's been contaminated by all the undignified emotion of the scene.

'I'll leave you to it,' he says to me. He looks down at Edie. 'Nice to meet you, then,' he says in a too-loud voice, as if she is mad, stupid and/or deaf.

She ignores him and continues to bawl into her open palms. I watch until Leon has left the cafe and is safely out of sight.

Then I turn back to Edie. I might have dealt with one difficult situation, but now I've got another one on my hands. I've never been much good at dealing with criers.

But when I look at Edie, her shoulders have stopped shaking. Her face is still pressed into her palms, but there's a gap in her fingers and the eye that's peering through it is quite dry. She parts her hands and looks furtively around.

'Is he gone?'

I blink, surprised by this turn of events. 'Uh, yeah. Looks like it.'

Edie moves her hands away from her face and flicks her hair out of her eyes. 'Thought that'd do the trick. Us British folk can't stand tears. We'd rather watch a public execution than a public breakdown.' She crinkles her nose and gives me such a mischievous grin that I can't help but laugh.

'That one after you then, is he?' she asks, nodding towards the chair where Leon had sat.

I stir my tea with the little wooden stirring stick. 'I don't know. In a way, sort of. But not really. I think he just likes attention. From anyone.' I think this is probably partly true.

Edie nods thoughtfully. 'Don't they all, my love. Don't they all. Straight away I clocked that he was nuisance. Those over-confident ones always are. Can never quite believe that there might be a time or a place when they're not welcome.'

I laugh again and Edie says, 'Oh well, think we've seen the back of him for today at any rate. Want a bit of cake?'

10

Over the next couple of hours Edie chats non-stop. She does mention my dad from time to time but not in the deliberate, sombre way she did earlier. She tells me that she doesn't have a job because she gave it up to look after James – 'cooking, cleaning, errands, paperwork' – so now she's supposed to be looking for work again but doesn't know where to start. We talk a lot about general things – telly, music, books.

After a while, Edie takes a big mouthful of cake, and says, 'Anyway, you seem to know much more about me than I do about you. Tell me about you!'

I feel surprised by the question, although I suppose it's a reasonable one. If the whole point of me being here is for her to see what's left of her wonderful James then it stands to reason that she'd want to get the measure of me. Only thing is, I'm not sure what to say.

I shrug. 'There's not much to tell, really.'

Edie looks at me over the top of her mug. 'Bet there is.'

I give her a few dull details – tell her that I'm basically quite average at school, OK grades but nothing special, not wildly popular but not really unpopular either. Just unremarkable.

'What else?' Edie says.

I shrug again.

Edie smiles and rolls her eyes. 'OK. Let's play a game. I ask the questions, you do the answers. No pauses. No shrugging. Just go, go, go. OK?'

I'm about to shrug again but Edie holds up a warning finger and I laugh and let my shoulders relax. 'OK, go on then.'

'Favourite film.'

'Uh . . .'

'No thinking! Go with your gut. Favourite film?'

'*Forrest Gump.*'

'Favourite song?'

'Uh . . .'

'Favourite colour?'

'Yellow . . . "Hallelujah" . . .'

Edie scrunches her nose up. 'Your favourite song is "Yellow"? By Coldplay? Fair enough, each to their own . . .'

I laugh. 'No! Yellow for the colour! My favourite song is "Hallelujah".'

Edie eyes me suspiciously. 'Which version?'

'Leonard Cohen.'

She smiles. 'Excellent answer.'

'Lifetime ambition?'

'Uh . . .'

'Quick, don't think, just speak!'

'Go to the moon!'

'Really?'

'No! I just said it! I'd hate to go to the moon. All that nothingness. Ugh.'

Edie smiles. 'Oh, me too, love. Can't think of anything worse. So what is it really then?'

'My ambition?' I shrug. 'No idea really.'

'What will you do when you finish school? Must be soon, surely?'

I nod. 'Mum wants me to stay on and do my A-levels but I don't know if there's any point.'

'What would you study?'

'Mum wants me to do sciences or maths. Or a language, at least.'

'And what do you want?'

I shake my head. 'I don't know. Something fun. And easy. Art, I suppose.' I grin sheepishly. 'But that's pointless. No one ever got a job from studying art.'

'James did art at university.'

'Really?' I'm surprised by this, but probably more surprised that I didn't know it.

Edie nods. 'Yep. First class degree in Fine Art. And he didn't do too badly out of it . . . although I guess he didn't imagine himself sketching out cartoons for washing powder adverts back when he was studying the works of Monet and Picasso and the bloke who cut off his nose.'

I frown. 'I think it was his ear? I think he cut off his ear. Not his nose. '

Edie waves her hand absently. 'Oh well, yes. Ear. Nose. Tongue. Whatever.' There's an awkward pause and I wonder if correcting her like that makes me a bit of a dick. But then Edie just does a little smile and says, 'General knowledge isn't really my strong point.'

'Mine neither.' I grin and we both laugh.

We're quiet for a moment and then I suddenly find myself saying, 'Have you got a photo? Of my dad?'

I'm just curious really – about how much he will have changed since the one photo I have of him, where I'm sitting on his lap with Mum next to us on holiday somewhere. That must've been taken twelve, thirteen years ago.

Edie seems taken aback by the sudden request, but she reaches for her bag. 'Yes. Yes, of course.' She opens her purse and slides a photo out from where it's tucked under the credit cards. She pushes it over the table to me.

I look down at his face. He looks the same. Older, thinner, greyer. But definitely the same. I look into his eyes in the photo and suddenly very clearly remember looking into those eyes in real life and I feel weird to think that those alive eyes are now dead eyes. He was there, sitting on that bench in that garden, but now he's gone. He's nowhere at all.

'Are you OK?' Edie asks.

'Yeah.' It comes out too loud. 'Yeah, fine.' I pass the photo back to her.

'You can keep that one . . . if you like?'

'Nah.' I shake my head quickly. 'You're all right.'

If Edie is surprised by my refusal she doesn't show it. She just tucks the photo back into her purse.

I think we both sense that our meeting is coming to an end. We finish our drinks and head out into the rain. Outside the cafe door, we say our goodbyes – 'nice to meet you', 'have a safe journey' – but neither of us says 'have a nice life' or anything as final as that. I suppose it's not the done thing, to say out

57

loud how neither of you is that bothered about seeing each other again. I wonder if this is what it's like when you come to the end of a bad date.

Edie turns left to head up towards the high street and the station. That's the direction I need to head too, but I hang back, pretending I need to go the other way so we don't have any accidental awkward meetings as we make our way home. I watch her walk down the road, battling against the wind with her giant umbrella, her layers of skirts billowing around her legs. I realise I feel like I've known her a lot longer than a couple of hours.

I find George and Sienna on my door-step when I get home. Literally sitting on the door-step.

'What are you doing?' I call as I head up the drive.

Sienna stands up. 'Your mum wouldn't let us in! She came right up to the window, looked at us, then just turned around and went away again! I'm sorry to say it, Anna, but I think she's gone rather mad.'

'Christ.' I realise she's kept to her word and stubbornly refused to admit any callers, even ones she knows. She can be so pathetic. 'Sorry.'

'It's OK,' she says. 'We've used the time well.'

She spins George around to show me the back of his head, where she's carefully woven his hair into tiny, neat, dreadlock-style plaits. George just shrugs and shakes his head in a 'what can you do?' kind of way.

I let us in the house and they traipse after me into the kitchen. I notice George is carrying a Tupperware box.

'What's that?'

He puts it on the kitchen table. 'We made it. For you. Because you're mad at us and we want you to get over it.'

'Am I?'

'Yes,' he says. 'You walked right out of my place in a proper fat strop and you didn't even have your second cake.'

Sienna shoots him a glare. 'He *means*, we made it for you because you've had a horrible week and we're your friends.'

I can't be bothered to question that. I can't be bothered to talk at all. I realise I'm exhausted. Today has been kind of draining.

'What is it, then? What have you made me?'

George looks at Sienna. She gives him the nod and he peels off the lid.

It's a cake. It's iced in white, with black letters sketched on top. *you're well moody but we don't mind*

I look from the cake to their faces and back again. They hover next to the table nervously.

'It's like one of the badges,' George explains. 'A badge cake.'

I raise an eyebrow. 'An *offensive* badge cake?'

George shoots Sienna a little alarmed look. 'It's a joke!' she protests. 'Banter! It's why you love us! We're all about the banter!'

'So what kind of cake is it?' I pick a bit of icing off and put it in my mouth.

'Chocolate,' George says quickly. 'Like, super chocolately.'

'Crack it open, then.' I pass him a knife and he gives me a relieved smile.

When George has cut us cake and Sienna has made us tea, we sit at the table. They both still seem a little on edge and I

59

wonder if my leaving George's last night was more dramatic than I realised. I decide to ask this now.

George pauses. I can't tell if he's chewing or considering what to say. Probably both.

'It's not really just that. It's more how you've been all week, mate. Like since that letter from the woman about your . . . you know. You've been funny. Changeable. Weird.'

'Really?' I'm genuinely surprised.

Sienna nods vigorously. 'You always say, "I'm fine, it's nothing." Always. But sometimes you should just tell us, you know. Stop being brave!'

I laugh at the very idea of me being brave but then I consider what she's said for a moment. I *have* felt on edge this week – tense, a knotted foreboding feeling in my stomach – but I thought I'd hidden it pretty well. Obviously not, though. And I didn't really think it was to do with the letter at all. Truth is, I thought it was more to do with Leon. But maybe it was to do with the letter. After all, the Leon business isn't new. That whole shitstorm has been dragging on for months.

'I met her,' I announce suddenly. 'Just now.' I hadn't planned to tell them.

'Who?'

'Edie Southwood.'

George frowns. 'You mean that mental –'

Sienna cuts him off. 'The lady who wrote the letter?'

I nod.

Both of them are looking at me. I take another bite of cake.

'And . . .?' Sienna prompts.

I chew for a moment. 'I don't know. It was weird.'

Sienna winces and nods sympathetically. 'Well, she did sound a bit weird in the letter . . . all that bit about ghosts. And her bottom.'

I sigh. 'I didn't say *she* was weird. It was just . . . I don't know. I don't want to talk about it. It's done now, anyway.'

George seems relieved that I don't want to go over the meeting with them, to analyse it in minute detail. 'Oh well,' he says with a reassuring smile. 'You never have to see her again, do you?'

'No,' I agree. 'Guess not.'

11

It's after school on Friday and George has roped me and Sienna into going down to the seafront with him to help his ongoing badge business project.

Much to our surprise, George has managed to shift a good chunk of the six hundred badges he made and with everything going so well he's decided it's time to extend his product range. As well as badges, he now has on offer little metal key rings and, weirdly, skin-tight black vests, the kind of thing you might wear to a yoga class if you were that way inclined. George has managed to do a few key ring deals, but as yet, he hasn't had a single taker for the vests.

'I think the vests were a mistake,' I told him after a week of unsuccessful pitching. 'People don't wear vests. Unless they're like . . . in a German pop video or something. You should've got proper T-shirts.'

George sighed. 'Anna. This is not about what people do *now*. I'm not interested in now. I'm creating new behaviours, new fashions. What I'm doing here is creating a brand so cool, so cutting edge, that people will *start* to wear vests just to be a part of it. I'm not a trend follower, Anna. I am a trend-*setter*.'

Sienna walked past at that moment and ruffled George's ginger hair. 'I've always thought you were more of a red setter really, Georgie.'

George ignored our laughter. 'And the other thing is,' he went on, 'vests only cost me two quid a piece. T-shirts are a fiver. I'm not made of money, you know. I'm already having cash flow issues as it is.'

Anyway, George has decided that school is not the market for his trend-setting skin-tight vests, and so the three of us are down at the beach, standing behind a fold-up table he's nicked from his parents' shed, laying out badges, key rings and neatly folded vests, ready for the onslaught of customers.

'Tourists, Anna,' George explained when I questioned his choice of venue. 'Tourists are just looking for things to spend money on. Have you seen the crap they sell in souvenir shops? Those guys would literally buy bottles of air if it was packaged right. And if we're looking for tourists, we need to be on the beach.'

George has insisted that we both model as much product as possible so at half past four on an October afternoon I find myself parading up and down the promenade shouting, 'Vests and key rings and badges, key rings and badges and vests!' wearing a skin-tight vest pulled over my hoody, the words *worse than anchovies* emblazoned across my chest. I am ridiculous.

Sienna and I are tasked with drumming up business from opposite ends of the prom; George is manning the table, ready to package up the products and receive the anticipated influx of cash. He's doing his sales bit too, of course, and as I wander down to the beach, I can hear him calling, 'Roll up! Roll up! Souvenirs! Gifts! Something for everyone!' like someone at a Victorian fun fair.

A hundred metres away, I hear Sienna burst into song – something from *Mary Poppins* I think, although I'm not sure what that has to do with anything.

'Music is the way to people's hearts,' she told me seriously on the walk down here. 'We have to sing to them. Any songs, all songs. Trust me, they'll love it. We'll enchant them with our voices!'

Fairly certain that no one is very likely to be enchanted by my voice, I jump down onto the pebbles and meander around, trying to catch people's eye, hoping they'll ask me about my vest rather than me having to try to strike up conversation with them. Most people barely give me a second look though, so I'm forced to stop them, ask them if they like my vest and then, regardless of their answer, point them in the direction of George's makeshift market stall. It's a truly painful process.

Most people start shaking their heads and saying, 'No, sorry,' when I've only got as far as 'Excuse me' but if I manage to hold their attention as far as the 'do you like my vest?' bit, they start to visibly freak out and walk in the opposite direction. They probably think I'm part of some kind of hidden camera show. Maybe I *am* part of some hidden camera show and George has set this whole thing up to make me look like a twat. I wouldn't be surprised.

I look back towards George's stall. He's now moved on from his *roll up, roll up* chant and seems to be shouting out all sorts of random cockney phrases. In fact, I'm not sure it's even cockney. It might just be gibberish. 'Apples and pears, up the stairs! Butcher's hook, take a look! Jump and jive, twenty-five!'

And the weirdest thing is, it seems to be working. A small crowd of Japanese tourists have gathered nearby to take photos and videos, and one or two are even holding up vests against themselves and showing them to their friends. With George distracted, I decide I've earned a break and I duck into a chip shop to get a drink.

I buy a can of Fanta and perch on one of the bollards near the entrance to the pier. A middle-aged man stops in front of me. He looks me up and down, then he says, 'I like anchovies, actually,' before marching on.

'Me too, mate,' I mutter under my breath and gaze down the pier, watching little kids pelt up and down on their scooters, and seagulls swoop overhead, trying to dive-bomb people for chips.

As I look towards the amusement arcade, I notice someone duck down suddenly and disappear behind one of those boards with cut-out circles where the faces should be. I keep watching, waiting for the face to appear in the hole ready for the photo opportunity, but it doesn't. This strikes me as strange – either the person is a midget or they're ducking down. Hiding. Then I see the umbrella poking out the bottom. Black and white spots. It takes me a minute to remember where I've seen it before but then it comes to me:

Edie.

12

I stand up, bin my Fanta can and make my way onto the pier and over to the board. As I turn the corner, I look around and see it is indeed Edie. She's crouched down, peering anxiously around the other edge. She hasn't noticed me approach at all.

'Edie?'

She jerks her head up, shocked. 'Oh! Anna! Hi!'

She stands up, smoothing down her skirts. She's wearing at least three or four again – this time teamed with a knitted woollen jacket in multi-coloured stripes.

'What are you doing?' I try to make the question sound light and curious rather than accusatory.

'Just . . . just, my shoelace . . .' We both look down at her shoes. She's wearing Wellington boots. No laces in sight.

'Right, OK, then . . .' I say, frowning.

She closes her eyes for a brief second, gathering herself, then she breathes out.

'So I'm lying,' she says. 'Obviously.'

'Yes,' I agree and we both look down at her boots again.

'I was hiding.' She looks sheepish and spins her umbrella

on its point. She looks like a little girl who's been caught stealing biscuits.

'Hiding? From what?'

'From you!' she laughs suddenly. It sounds high-pitched, maybe a bit mad.

I frown, confused. 'How do you mean?'

Edie stops laughing. 'Sorry,' she says. 'Sorry. I just was here . . . you know, walking and then I saw you, over there.' She points to the bollard where I'd been sitting with my Fanta. 'And I thought, if you see me you're going to think I'm stalking you or something so . . . I don't know. I didn't think. I thought it was best if you didn't see me.'

'Oh, right.' I rub the space between my eyebrows with my finger. I'm not sure what to make of it. 'I wouldn't have thought you were stalking me. I don't think I would, anyway.'

Edie sighs. 'Yes. Yes I suppose that's true. And now I've just made myself look mad!' She puts her hands on her hips and looks up to the sky, shaking her head. 'Oh, for heaven's sake, Edith. Why can't you just be normal?' She laughs again but she seems sad somehow. Suddenly she peers at me closely. 'What's wrong with anchovies?'

Then it's my turn to laugh. I shake my head and look down at my vest. 'Honestly no idea.'

I go over to the railing that runs along the length of the prom and point towards where George is stationed. 'Look.'

Edie joins me.

'That's George,' I tell her. 'He sells stuff. Weird stuff, sometimes. He's kind of an entrepreneur. At the moment he's selling these. So I'm helping.'

'Right.' Edie holds her hand up to shield her eyes from the sun and we both watch while George shakes hands with an old man with a long, white beard and passes him what looks like a handful of vests.

'They're not all about anchovies,' I add. 'Some of them say other things.'

Edie chuckles, then she puts her hand down and turns to look at me. 'You know what, I'm going to get some candy floss,' she says. 'Isn't that the point of the seaside? Do you want some? My treat!' She's already heading off in the direction of the kiosk.

'Uh, yeah. Sure,' I call after her.

Edie brings two bags of candy floss and we walk along the pier to the quiet benches at the end that look out towards the open sea. 'You're probably wondering what I'm doing here at all,' Edie says.

I don't know that I am, really. It's a popular seaside town; lots of people come for whatever reason. But I get the feeling Edie wants to tell me why she's here so I play along. 'I guess, a bit,' I say.

'To be honest with you, Anna, I don't know what I'm doing. I wake up in the morning and I think, "What shall I do today?" and I don't even know. So I just go places . . . here, the countryside . . . wherever. I like it here – where James used to live. I just roam around, killing time. And I think, what did I do before? What did I do before James? Who *was* I?'

We're quiet for a moment. It seems weird to me, the idea of putting so many eggs into one boyfriend-shaped basket. But then, what do I know about anything? 'No more luck with the job search, then?'

She shakes her head. 'I'm just no good at it. I go into places and I say, "Do you have any jobs?" but I already know they don't want me before I've even got the words out.'

'Do you give them your CV and all that?'

Edie takes a sheet of crumpled paper out of her handbag. She passes it to me and I smooth it out. At the top it says *Edith Southwood* CV in neat blue Biro. It's underlined twice with careful ruled lines. Underneath it is a simple list of job titles and dates, just ordinary stuff – waitressing, doing the till in a gift shop, that kind of thing. At the bottom she's written the name of her school. Next to it it says 'NO GCSEs' in neat block capitals. That bit makes me laugh out loud.

'What?' She looks at me anxiously. 'Is it my spelling?'

I feel bad so I stop laughing. 'It's just very honest,' I say.

'Oh.' Edie looks down at the paper. 'I didn't know about that GCSE bit, but I thought it was probably better they found out sooner rather than later.'

'Maybe you should type it up?' I suggest. I remember when I worked at Martina's: if anyone handed her a CV with so much as a font she didn't like the look of, she'd screw it up and chuck it in the bin. 'No good,' she'd say. 'No attention to the looks. Is no good for me.'

'I tried,' Edie says looking pained. 'I *did* try. I used the computer in the library but I couldn't get everything to look right . . . that little flashy line keeps jumping around and making me write in all the wrong places so I just gave up in the end. How does anyone ever bother with a computer? It takes hours,

69

searching all the buttons for the letter you want!'

It's kind of funny but she seems so distressed by the whole thing it would be mean to laugh.

'I could do it for you, if you like?'

Edie looks at me, obviously surprised at the offer – I'm quite surprised at it myself, as it happens. Then she smiles. 'You mean, type it up? For me?'

'Yeah, sure. It won't take long.'

'Oh, Anna!' She takes hold of my hand. 'That would be wonderful!'

We finish our candy floss and bin the plastic bags. We stroll around the end of the pier, watching the boats and the surfers bob about in the waves. Edie chats some more and I'm happy to mostly listen.

She tells me an animated story about the time she accidentally got caught up in a fire drill at the cinema and how she'd got confused and thought some genuine emergency was unfolding.

'So there I am, herding children, trying to make sure everyone's safe, you know, trying to be useful – when this manager bloke comes up to me and has to say, "Er, madam, it's just a drill. No need to alarm the public." And there's me, taking a note of kids' names in case any parents are missing anyone, looking like a right plonker!'

She drops in some serious stuff too – about how both her parents were dead by the time she was sixteen and how she lived in a homeless hostel for a bit as a teenager – but the way she talks, focusing on the silly parts, her West Country farmer accent in full swing, means that somehow everything she says is kind of hilarious.

The conversation turns back to George and his stall, and Edie is keen to know all the different offensive slogans he's come up with. I reel off the ones I can remember and Edie seem to find them all totally hysterical. Her special favourite seems to be *trumpet nose* and I promise to try to get her a badge if I can.

Then, right on cue, George appears. 'There you are!' he calls, heading up the pier towards us.

I amble over to meet him. 'Hi. Yeah. Sorry. I'm still wearing it though.' I look down at the anchovies vest. 'Still modelling.'

'Not much good down here where there aren't any people though, is it? But never mind. It's gone well, I must say. I done some good trade this afternoon. Sienna managed to get an entire male voice choir to buy a vest each – they reckon they're going to wear them at some gig in Malta! Tell you what, if they do, it'll be *outstanding* publicity for the brand. Anyway, she's hanging around to sing along with them in the bandstand or something but I'm heading off for the evening. You coming? Or are you . . . busy?'

He looks pointedly at Edie. She looks back at George. I have no choice but to introduce them.

'This is George,' I tell Edie. 'With the badges. And the key rings and the vests. George, this is Edie.'

'Oh, *Edie*,' George says, giving me a look that says, 'so this is the psycho?' and also, 'what the hell are you playing at, sitting here with her?' Luckily he doesn't say either of these things out loud.

'I'm very impressed with your products,' Edie says politely.

'Oh right, yeah. Thanks.' George rubs the back of his head awkwardly. Then he turns back to me. 'So, you coming then or what?'

'Oh yes, you must get on,' Edie says. 'I need to get home anyway. Lovely to see you though, Anna.'

'Uh, yeah, you too. I'll text you when I've done your CV.'

'Oh yes! Thank you so much.' Edie looks around her like she's worried she's left something behind. 'And if, you know, you can't be bothered or whatever then that's fine . . . no pressure . . . Anyway . . . must go! Bye, bye now!' She seems in a hurry to get away suddenly and half walks, half trots towards the pier exit.

'Bye, then . . .' I call after her, but she's already gone.

George looks down the pier, watching her go. 'So that was the crazy then, was it?'

I roll my eyes. 'She's not a crazy, George. She's just a bit . . .'

'Unstable? Unhinged?' He's grinning. He's winding me up on purpose. There's no point rising to it.

I shake my head. 'She's just kind of lost, I think.'

George makes a face. 'Well, I still think you should steer clear, mate. People with issues can be a right ball-ache.'

13

The following week, Leon ambushes me after geography. He steps out in front of me like he's been lying in wait, like a mountain lion stalking its prey.

'Anna! When can I take you out? We need to get a date in the diary.'

The only diary I keep is my homework diary and anyway, I really do not want to go anywhere with Leon. He's been asking to 'take me out' for weeks though. I'm running out of acceptable excuses.

'Uh, whenever. Any time.'

Leon holds his hand out in front of him as if to usher me along the corridor. I go ahead and he walks along beside me, standing slightly too close so our upper arms are touching unnecessarily.

'Well, listen,' he goes on. 'I've got tickets to this thing on Wednesday . . . a literary thing, you know. A panel. The list of speakers probably won't mean anything to you but there are some big names. It's quite an opportunity, for those of us in the business. Why don't you come? We can eat first – I'll book us a table at that gorgeous little Italian place in town.'

I really, really do not want to go anywhere with Leon, Italian or otherwise.

'OK. Sounds good.'

'Excellent, excellent. Good girl. I'll pick you up about six! And as I say, the restaurant is quite a *nice* one, if you know what I mean . . .'

I look at him blankly.

He sighs. 'I *mean*, you might want to smarten yourself up a bit. Wear a nice little dress, sort your hair out . . . that kind of thing.'

His eyes flick up to my hair, which as usual I've pulled back into a ponytail so I don't have to worry about it. It's all I can do not to punch him in the gut.

I spend the whole of Wednesday desperately trying to think how I can get out of the evening. I know I could pretend I was ill or that some kind of emergency has come up, but I also know I'd only be putting off the inevitable. Even if I could put Leon off this time, he'll still be on at me again soon enough, nagging me to put another 'date in the diary'. I seriously wish that I could just tell Leon Jakes-Field to never speak to me again, to disappear, to jump into a disused well. In a way, I'm tempted to try it – to just take a chance and brace myself for the consequences – but I know that would be a stupid, reckless thing to do.

Leon rings the doorbell bang on six o'clock. He's wearing a full-on three-piece suit – waistcoat, tie, the whole shebang. He's smeared so much gel on his hair I reckon I could knock on it like a helmet if I wanted. I've ignored his instructions about wearing a 'nice little dress'. Even if I had one, I'd draw the line at letting Leon's control over me go that far. If he's disappointed by my appearance, he hides it well.

'Anna! You look nice. Sweet top.' He reaches out to touch the fabric and I instinctively pull away.

As we walk into town it's a bit cold, so I tuck my hands inside the sleeves of my jacket. Leon notices and makes a show of draping his suit jacket over my shoulders. He then tries to walk with his arm around me but thankfully we keep getting out of step so he's forced to give up and let go.

At one point we see two people from school – Callum Steward and Madison Porter. Callum and Madison are kind of a celebrity couple in our year. Their on-off relationship has been dragging on for so long that they even have their own couple nickname: 'Stewport'. They're walking hand in hand and Callum is saying something to make Madison giggle. As we approach them, I step away from Leon and bend down. 'Shoelace . . .' I mutter and fiddle around with my shoe. I keep my head bowed until they're safely past us. Luckily they seemed too caught up in each other to notice me. I really don't want it getting around school that Leon and I have been on a proper date.

We arrive at Marco's Fine Italian Restaurant, where the table cloths are crisp and white and smart waiters glide silently around us. It seems expensive, and a quick glance at the menu confirms this. You could get a week of canteen lunches for the price of one dish here. Still, I decide, since I'm going to have to go through this whole painful evening, I might as well get something out of it. I order smoked salmon, steak and a cheese board.

While we eat, Leon drones on about his creative writing club and a short story he's submitted to a magazine and how he feels like he's 'really at a turning point now'.

I quickly get bored of pretending to listen. I start off saying, 'yeah' and 'oh really?' at regular intervals but as I tune further and further out I stop saying anything at all. Then suddenly, Leon puts down his fork and says, 'For god's sake Anna, I've brought you to this nice place, do you think you could at least do me the courtesy of listening to what I'm saying?'

I blink, taken aback. This is the first time Leon has spoken like this to me. He's often hinted when I've done something to displease him, implied what he'll do if I don't go along with what he wants, but he's always done it with that serene, sinister smile of his, so that afterwards I'm not even sure that it happened at all. I feel genuinely alarmed. I must've really annoyed him for him to snap like that. I need to up my game. I can't afford to let myself get complacent.

'Sorry, Leon,' I say, my face a picture of contrition, 'I am listening, of course. It's just . . . I've got a lot on my mind.'

Leon leans towards me, his fingers pushed together at the tips. 'Oh, Anna,' he says, shaking his head sadly. 'It's your dad again, isn't it? Are you *still* thinking about it?'

In actual fact, I'm not still thinking about it, not really, but the way he says 'still' like that – like I really should be over it by now, like a dead parent is some pathetic, trivial mishap – winds me right up. I make myself take two deep breaths. I need to be careful here. I give him a shrug and look away towards the window. It's the best I can do. Better to say nothing.

Leon places his hand on mine. It takes all my willpower not to shake it off.

'You'll get there,' he says, his eyes full of that unbearable smugness masquerading as sympathy. 'You'll get there.'

Near the end of the meal, Leon looks up and says, 'Do you think about the future, Anna?'

I'm surprised. Leon doesn't ask me questions very often. He prefers that I listen while he speaks. He definitely doesn't ask me big open questions like this one, questions that make it seem as if he's actually interested in what I've got to say.

'Uh . . . sometimes, I suppose.'

'I can see us being together in the future,' he says, with a knowing look. 'Can't you?'

'Uh . . .'

'I think it makes sense,' he goes on. 'I know things aren't perfect between us at the moment, but I think in ten years' time we'll look back on these days and laugh. One of the reasons I'm so loyal to you, Anna, is because I can see potential. I know that although you can be wilful now, you have the makings of a wonderful, supportive wife. I look at you, and do you know what I see? I see a butterfly, just waiting to burst out of its cocoon. I have a strong feeling that when you're eighteen or nineteen, you're going to wake up one day, you're going to look in the mirror and you're going to say, "Wow, that is one attractive woman." I know you can't imagine it now, Anna, but I've got a knack for seeing through the obvious, seeing past what other people see. In a few years' time, the last of that puppy fat will have dropped off, you'll start styling your hair, a bit of decent foundation . . . You wait and see. It'll be a real Cinderella transformation.' He leans back in his chair and grins widely, obviously pleased with this little analysis. 'Just promise me one thing,' he says with a mock conspiratorial tone, 'when you get there, you'll remember who saw you first?' He gives me an exaggerated wink and points at his chest with his thumb.

'Sure,' I say through gritted teeth. 'I'll remember.'

14

When the bill comes, Leon flips open the little leather folder. He does a theatrical wince and chuckles. 'That steak of yours – woah! Good thing for you it's my treat, eh?' He laughs again and I make myself smile sweetly.

'It's very kind of you, Leon.'

The writers' panel discussion is being held in the basement of a bar called The Centipede, just back from the seafront. As we make our way there, I notice two burly bouncers on the door. I assume Leon has prepared for this, but when we reach the entrance, the smaller of the two moves in front of us, blocking our path.

'ID, please,' he says, his eyes focused on Leon.

Leon looks faintly amused. 'What for, exactly?'

'Your age, sunshine. I'm buggered if you're eighteen.'

Leon rubs his spotty chin as if stroking an imaginary beard. 'Well no, quite. I'm not eighteen. But I do have tickets for the panel event.'

The bouncer looks unimpressed. 'You what?'

Leon lets out an exasperated sigh and reaches for the tickets from the inside pocket of his coat. 'The writers' panel event?

Henry McCain? He's quite well known, although I realise he's probably not *your* cup of tea.'

I reckon that if I was the bouncer, I'd shut the door in Leon's face right about now, but then I suppose security staff are used to putting up with bigger nuisances than Leon. The bouncer leans inside and calls over to the barman.

'Oi, Fabio, you heard about this event? Henry Mc-something?'

Fabio comes over. He frowns slightly, thinking for a moment, but then he nods. 'Yeah, yeah. Rings a bell. Basement.'

'What's the situation with under-agers?'

Fabio shrugs. 'Well, there ain't no bar down there.'

The bouncer sighs. He's obviously already wasted more time and effort than he would've liked on a little weasel like Leon. He stands aside.

'Straight downstairs, then. Go anywhere near the bar and you're out on your arse.'

We step inside and Leon turns back to me and says, 'Well, one thing's perfectly clear and that's that he will never amount to anything more than hired muscle. What an absolute imbecile.'

Leon makes no effort to lower his voice as he delivers this assessment and I look nervously back at the bouncer to see if he's going to say something, but he's just leaning against the door-frame, rolling a cigarette.

The basement has been set up with rows of plastic chairs facing a simple wooden table where three people are already sitting, sipping drinks and chatting amongst themselves. I gather these are the writers. We take our seats and Leon leans in close to me and, in a low whisper, fills me in on who's who.

'Dylan O'Shea on the left there is a mid-list Irish author. He'll be talking about historical accuracy – or lack of – which is kind of his pet peeve. Moira Garratt, in the middle, she writes all sorts of far-fetched crime nonsense. She'll probably talk more than anyone would like – god knows why they invited her at all. She's frankly far more successful than she deserves to be. But the person I'm really interested in, the star of the show, is Henry McCain – the one on the right. He's something of a maverick – a great American genius, some say. I met him once a few years back at a book signing. I told him that I was a writer and he took quite some interest, I can tell you. We talked at length about something I was working on at the time and he said that when it was complete, we must talk again. And, Anna, when we'd finished talking, he gave me this wink, this little look, and I knew that that look was a kind of gentleman's agreement. I knew that what he was saying was that if I did what I said I would do, if I got it finished, he would help me out. He would make things happen. So –' Leon pulls himself up and straightens his jacket – 'tonight's the night. It's finished. It's perfect.'

'Can't your mum just help you?' I ask. 'She knows the right people, surely? Publishers and all that?'

Leon gives me a withering look. 'Well, yes, *obviously* my mother is incredibly well connected, but she's always made it clear that I have to succeed on my own merit. She won't give me any short cuts. And quite right too. It would be an insult for her to suggest I needed to rely on nepotism to make my mark on the world.'

'So you're going to try to speak to this Henry then? Do you think there'll be time for that – is that how these things work?'

'Well, not for everyone of course. He can't be expected to have a *tête-à-tête* with every Tom, Dick and Harry. But I'll find a quiet moment at the end, see if he wants to go for a coffee sometime.'

I look over at Henry McCain, with his bushy ginger beard and tweed jacket. The other two are chatting away merrily enough, but he's stopped joining in. He's just peering out at his audience, sipping at something that looks like whisky. He doesn't look very pleased to be here. I can't really see his mouth under all the facial hair but it looks a bit like he's doing a bit of a snarl.

When everyone's in their seat, a man from the front row, who I gather is in charge of proceedings, stands up to thank everyone for coming and to kick things off. The talk is actually quite interesting. As Leon said he would, the Irish guy talks about history and research and how he goes about checking his facts. I don't think Leon was quite fair to call it a pet peeve though – he's clearly quite dedicated to the accuracy of his work but I find it quite impressive.

Moira Garrat is much better than Leon gave her credit for, too. Her stories about working with the police and witnessing real crime scenes are kind of fascinating and the way she talks about the characters she's met – the bumbling old policemen, the keen young scientists – is hilarious. I make a note to check out her books next time I'm in the library. If anyone's a let-down on the panel, it's actually Henry McCain. It's like someone's forced him to be there and he's punishing them by being as surly and sarcastic as possible. Whenever one of the others tries to bring him into the discussion, he either cuts them down or makes a grumpy huffing noise. After a while they stop asking his opinions at all and he gazes moodily out into the space above our heads, occasionally scratching his beard or taking a sip of his drink.

I'm not sure Leon is listening at all. On several occasions I notice him peering inside his bag at a big wodge of paper he's brought with him. I realise that this must be it – his great work of genius, ready to show off to his idol. It's obvious that he doesn't have any interest in the talk at all. He's just waiting for it to be over so he can have his big moment. His one-to-one with Henry McCain.

After the main talk, there's a question and answer session. I tune out a bit at this point because lots of the people in the room seem to be asking very rambling, long-winded questions. It seems to me that some people aren't really asking questions at all – they're just putting up their hands to give their opinions on anything they feel like, most of the time on things that don't seem to be at all related to anything the panel have talked about.

After about ten minutes of this, Henry McCain points directly at where we're sitting and says, 'You, there. Kid in the festive waistcoat.' I look to my left and I'm surprised to see Leon's hand in the air. Surely he'd rather get this bit over with, let the masses file out so he can seize his moment with Henry McCain alone?

'Yes, yes, thank you,' he says. He gets to his feet, even though all the other question-askers had stayed seated. 'Leon Jakes-Field,' he says, his hand on his chest to show he's introducing himself. 'I was just wondering, Mr McCain, if the character of Julian in *The January Problem* was in any way based on yourself?'

Henry McCain takes a sip of his drink. Then he looks straight at Leon and says, 'Nice idea, kid, but he's a communist, a scientist and – sorry to spoil it for anyone who hasn't read it yet – a murderer. I am none of those things.' Then with one eyebrow raised, he adds, 'Yet.' A nervous laugh ripples through the audience.

'So, no, then?' Leon says, still on his feet.

Henry McCain sighs a weary sigh. 'No, son. I did not base Julian Horn on myself.' He says the words slowly and carefully like he's talking to an idiot.

As soon as the panel's moved on to the next question, Leon leans over to me. 'You see, what I was doing there was clever – obviously I didn't really want to know the answer to such a mundane, clichéd question, but I did want to give him the chance to have a look at me, to remember that we'd met. Right about now he'll be wondering what I'm doing here. You wait – he'll probably seek me out at the end to ask.'

15

Henry McCain does not seek Leon out at the end.

Instead, as soon as the session has ended, he gets to his feet and makes for the stairs, empty whisky glass in hand. As we're forbidden to go near the main bar, Leon obviously realises that Henry will be lost to him if he heads up the stairs, so he calls after him.

'Henry! Henry!'

Henry stops and turns around. He looks irritated, like he's noticed a fly buzzing around his ears. 'I said no signings at this one.'

'Oh no, no.' Leon takes a few steps towards him. 'I don't want a signing. It's Leon, Leon Jakes-Field?'

Henry frowns. 'What?'

'Leon Jakes-Field,' Leon repeats, undeterred. 'We met three years ago at the Edgecut Literary Festival. You'll remember – you signed my copy of *Never When How* and we talked about my work in progress – a coming-of-age novel about challenging conventional ideas of success in twenty-first century Britain?'

Henry just tips his head right back to try to get the last dregs of whisky from his glass.

'Anyway,' Leon goes on. 'I'm pleased to say that that work is now finished.' He reaches into his bag for his writing. 'You asked to see it.'

Leon holds it out but Henry lifts his hands away, almost as if he's afraid that by touching it he's committing himself to showing an interest. 'I can't imagine that I did, son,' he says. 'I'm not in the business of reading schoolboys' homework.'

With this comment, Henry turns and makes his unsteady way up the stairs to the bar. Leon charges after him and I follow just behind, interested to see how the scene is going to pan out.

Henry saunters over to the bar and places his glass down. 'I'll take a scotch on the rocks, please, barman.'

Leon's followed Henry over and is now standing at his elbow. 'I distinctly remember you said, "Keep up the good work, you'll have something worth looking at I'm sure".'

Henry shrugs and throws his drink back in one. 'Did I? I must've been feeling generous that day. Normally I tell them all the truth – that they haven't got a hope.' Henry laughs loudly at his own joke and a few people look over.

Leon ignores this last comment. 'Anyway, here it is. At least have a look at the first few chapters. You owe me that, surely?'

This is a step too far for Henry. 'Owe you? I tell you something, son, I don't owe you anything. You think you're the first jumped-up little school kid to dash off some lame-ass story about growing up and falling in love and finding out your mommy never really loved you? I can tell you, kid. I get this kind of crap day in, day out, everywhere I go. The sooner you realise there ain't one single thing that makes you better than all the other no-hopers and wannabes, the better.'

Leon just stands there, staring at the glass in Henry's hand, not saying anything. Then Henry turns around and calls over to the bouncers, still in position at the door.

'Security! Get rid of this little pipsqueak, would you? He's wasting my drinking time.'

As soon as the bouncer from earlier catches sight of Leon he's more than happy to step in. He seizes Leon by the elbow and frogmarches him out of the door. A few blokes gathered round the pool table look over at the commotion and laugh.

Outside, Leon is fuming. 'I honestly can't imagine what has got into him,' he tells me as he walks quickly down the road away from the bar. 'I mean, he drinks, obviously. You can see he's a drinker. But he's clearly one of those who has a total personality bypass as soon as he's had one too many. They shouldn't let them drink, I don't think. Not when people have paid for tickets.'

'Maybe he just wasn't that interested,' I say.

I didn't think that through before I said it – it just came out – but it doesn't strike me as a particularly controversial suggestion. Leon doesn't see it this way though.

He stops walking suddenly and spins around to face me. 'OK then, Anna, you tell me: tell me what you have ever achieved. What are *your* ambitions? What are you going to accomplish in the next five years to show the world what you're made of? Nothing, is the answer to all of those questions. Nothing. You sneer at me, you think you're better than me with your pathetic, giggling little friends, but I am already one hundred times more successful than you will ever be.'

'Why hang around with me, then?' I snap back. 'What exactly do you want from me, Leon? You say you like spending time with me, but you clearly don't even like me!'

I've forgotten about being careful now, and I genuinely want to know the answer. I know why I *have* to spend time with him, but if I'm so awful why does he *want* to spend time with me? He's the one who seeks me out, who invites me to things I don't want to go to. He's the one who just won't leave me the hell alone.

Leon just stands there, his eyes flashing with anger. Then he leans in close, so close I can smell the pepperoni pizza on his breath. It makes me want to puke. 'You just remember, Anna, that where you and I are concerned, what I say goes. You don't insult me. You don't make me look a fool. You do what I want, when I want. We're on my terms now. That is, unless you want the police turning up with an arrest warrant for attempted murder.'

This hits me hard. For all Leon's insinuation about what he knows and what he'll do if I don't do what he wants, this is the first time he has referred to our situation so explicitly. He sees the shock in my face and it seems to please him. He lets out a cold laugh.

'Aw, don't look so sad, Anna-Spanner,' he says in a mock cutesy voice.

He reaches into his jacket and takes out his wallet. He flips it open and holds it up for me to see. 'We make the perfect couple, don't you think?' I look at the wallet and realise I'm looking directly at my own face. Leon has somehow got hold of a photo of me and slid it into the clear window of his wallet, right next to a picture of himself.

The photo is from a year or so ago, when George and I were messing around with his dad's old Polaroid camera in my room. I'd kept the photo. It was in a pile in a drawer in my room. There weren't any copies. So what I can't work out is how exactly Leon has got hold of it. Then I remember the book that Leon left for me, and the one he took.

'You stole this from my room?' I'm furious. As if the book wasn't bad enough, I now find out that he's been rifling through my drawers, helping himself to photos.

Leon just smirks. 'It's like I say, Anna. We're on my terms.'

I go to swipe his wallet and retrieve the photo but he pulls it away and tucks it back inside his jacket.

The evening is over, I decide. I will not waste one more second with him. I turn sharply and walk quickly down the road towards the seafront.

'And, Anna,' he calls after me. 'You owe me £24.95 for that steak!'

16

The Saturday after my horrendous date with Leon, I know it's about time I got on with typing up Edie's CV as I promised.

I'm pretty sure she'd never follow it up – I could quite easily never see her again – but I'd feel guilty. There's something about the crumpled, handwritten sheet of paper and the way she's carefully listed all her achievements, each one underlined with a ruler, that makes my chest ache.

We had a lesson on this kind of stuff at school last year – CVs, job applications, interviews. I'd thought the whole thing was totally pointless and obvious – 'Don't put spelling mistakes in your CV', 'Don't wear your pyjamas to an interview' – but now, looking at the scrap of paper in my hands, I can't help but wonder if Edie could've done with going to a couple of those lessons.

Aside from the issues with the presentation, Edie's main problem seems to be her complete and unadulterated honesty. For each job, she's written exactly what she did; nothing more, nothing less.

First job: gift shop

Duties: Scan things in till, take customer's money, give change.

Second job: cafe

Duties: Pick up plates from table, carry to kitchen, wipe table.

The other thing that might be a problem is that, just as she told me at our first meeting, she gave up work soon after she met my father and hasn't had a job since. This is how she's explained that career gap:

No work

Made dinner and tidied house for boyfriend.

I boot up my laptop and open a new document. I know I told Edie I'd just type it up but I have a feeling that unless I make some more material changes, a smartened-up copy isn't going to get her any further than this version has. I decide that while I'm here, I may as well add a few creative flourishes to Edie's candid descriptions.

An hour later, Edie's CV is transformed.

For example:

Scan things in till, take customer's money, give change

has become:

Senior retail assistant in busy gift shop. I provided exemplary service to a range of customers, offered expert product advice, took full responsibility for visual merchandising and displays, and handled all business cash.

I'm particularly proud of my explanation of her recent career gap:

PA to busy advertising executive. I managed all aspects of his scheduling and appointments, dealt with administrative matters and handled all communications.

I'm not sure that everything is one hundred per cent truthful now, but I feel confident it's near enough. At any rate, I can't see that any future employers are really likely to check this stuff out. Especially as her most recent reference – the 'busy advertising executive' – is now dead.

I sit back and admire my handiwork. Now I just need to get the thing to Edie.

I pick up my phone and tap out a text.

Your CV is ready. What's your email address? I'll send it over.

Thirty seconds later the phone rings.

'Anna! Thank you so much! I didn't know if you'd really do it . . . I mean, not that I doubted you but I know you must be so busy and I wouldn't have bothered you or even minded if you'd decided you didn't have time and . . . well, anyway. Thank you! Now my email address . . . The thing is, I'm not really big on email to be perfectly honest with you, but there are a few things we can try . . .'

Edie reels off a few different strings of words but none of them can possibly be email addresses – they either don't have a domain name or don't include the @ symbol. One of them is just the URL for the BBC news website.

'Oh,' she says when I reject her last attempt. 'Maybe I don't have an email address then?' She sounds crestfallen.

I find it almost impossible to believe that anyone can just not have an email address, but then Edie isn't quite like other people.

'I could set you one up now . . .' I suggest.

'Right . . .' Edie says uncertainly. 'And would I . . . know how to use it?'

It's a good point. Edie seems particularly clueless when it comes to IT and I don't fancy the idea of becoming her on-call technical support, having to hold her hand every time she wants to read an email or change her password.

'Well, maybe I can just post you some copies, then? Or give them to you when you're next down?'

Edie seems relieved. 'Oh yes, that sounds easier. Don't want it all getting lost down the wires.'

I laugh, but then I realise she isn't joking so I stop.

'Listen,' she says. 'I'm going to be down your way next week, at the Showbar – do you know it? My friend's in a band – gypsy folk, it is. Or is it gypsy jazz? You know the kind of thing . . . violins, panpipes, accordions. Anyway, they're doing a show – a "gig" – next week. On Halloween! A Halloween special. I've said I'd go but I could do with some company. I don't really like . . . you know. I mean, I still haven't got used to doing things on my own. As you're local, well, you could come. Do you think? Or not?'

'Uh, sure.' It was something about Edie's way of speaking – that farmy accent. The way she always seemed so unsure about everything. It made it hard to turn her down. It made me feel guilty.

'Oh!' She seems surprised, like she'd expected me to turn her down. 'Really? Oh, brilliant, that's brilliant news.'

Edie gives me instructions about tickets and where to meet. It's all a bit rambling and she contradicts herself several times but we eventually seem to have a plan and we end the call. When I've put my phone down, I look at her CV and think about what a funny person she is.

I wonder if this will be our last meeting.

17

Halloween – the day of Edie's friend's gig – falls on a Friday and over lunch that day, George and Sienna are making plans for a horror film marathon.

'So, I was thinking,' George says, 'tonight could be the night to unleash *The Beast*.'

'What beast?' Sienna and I ask at the same time.

'*The* Beast. The film. You know, that Japanese one I've been telling you about for ages.'

I try to remember which one he means. George tells us about a lot of stuff; only some of it is worth listening to. 'Didn't you say it was like, illegal or something?'

'Not illegal, just unrated. So, like, so completely mentally hideous that the film certificate people couldn't even watch it all the way through so they couldn't give it a rating.'

'But Japanese, though?' Sienna says. 'Does that mean it's got subtitles? Or is it dubbed? I hate both.'

George shakes his head.

'What, NEITHER?' Sienna looks unimpressed. 'So it's just a film *in* Japanese? Great. We won't have a bloody clue what's going on.'

George just shrugs. 'Dude, it's about a man who gets his guts ripped out by a mutant wolf. It's not exactly big on dialogue.'

'Did you know,' Sienna goes on, 'that in Japan, they wear toilet slippers. You have to put on special slippers to go to the toilet. To make sure you don't wee on your feet. It's a fact.'

'Yeah?' George says without much interest. He mops up some baked bean sauce with a chip.

'Yes,' Sienna confirms. 'So I will come, George; I will come and watch your terrible film, but only if you provide toilet slippers. Out of respect to the Japanese.'

'I'll see what I can do.' George stands up and picks up his tray. 'Come over about seven, yeah? Archie will be out by then so we'll have my room to ourselves.'

'I can't make it tonight,' I say quickly, not meeting either of their eyes. 'Got to do something with my mum.'

The other two exchange a look but if they don't believe me they don't say anything.

I didn't deliberately decide to keep my night out with Edie a secret from them, but I know it will be easier not to tell them. I know George will make some sarcastic comment about Edie being a nutter and Sienna will probably come over all melodramatic and ask me if I really think it's 'safe' to encourage someone with 'emotional issues'. Anyway, it's all immaterial. I'm not going to see Edie again after today so what's the point in bringing it up?

At seven o'clock, I'm in the designated meeting spot, just next to the entrance to the underpass that leads to the seafront. Just like with our first meeting at Martina's, I feel nervous about whether she'll actually arrive or not. I'm not sure why

I care – I'm still not sure if I actually want to go to this gig with her or not, or if I'm just doing it out of guilt – but as each person emerges from the underpass and it's not Edie, I feel a little sinking of disappointment, and then panic that I'm going to be stood up.

She eventually appears from behind me. I hear her before I see her.

'Anna! Oh, Anna! I'm so sorry!'

I turn to look at her. She's a striking sight. She's wearing her usual layers and layers of skirts, with a frilly white blouse on top, but instead of a coat she has a long black velvet cape. She's powdered her face very pale – white, almost – and her eyes are circled with heavy black eyeliner. Her lipstick is a deep, dark red. I genuinely have no idea whether this is just how she dresses for a night out or if she's come in Halloween gear for the occasion – something about the cape and red lipstick is definitely a bit Dracula. But it's not really polite to straight-out ask someone if they're in fancy dress or not, so I just say hello in the normal way and we make our way to the gig.

I've never been inside the Showbar before, but I like it at once. The walls have all been left as exposed brick, but they're dotted with posters of some of the bands who have played there over the years. There are candles on all the tables and a web of fairy lights hanging across the back wall. The whole place feels like a little magical cave. All around us people seem to be chatting easily with each other, either standing at the bar or at one of the many round tables spread across the floor.

Edie and I find an empty seat near the back of the room. Edie gets us drinks and as we sit and wait for the band to start, several people at nearby tables start casual conversations with us about the venue and weather and the band we're about to see. If I was with George and Sienna I know we'd be making faces at each other, complaining about all these random weirdos talking to us uninvited, but at the moment, here with Edie, it seems fine. I'm still not totally sure that Edie isn't a bit mad or even what I'm doing here at all, but for now, sitting here in the dim flickery light, sipping my Coke with the cheerful violin music playing in the background, I feel perfectly relaxed.

Edie's friend's band – The Hootwhistles – turn out to be really good. I'm not exactly a connoisseur of music but they're like nothing I've ever heard before. Their main singer, a tiny woman dressed in a fairy outfit, bounces around the stage like a firefly, while behind her, three chunky-bearded men play everything from a banjo to a cheese grater. Edie gets really into it. At first she's just clapping along, but later she gets to her feet and starts dancing next to our table, kicking out her legs and holding her skirts up around her knees. Although I can't quite bring myself to join in – I'm not sure I'm really a dancing kind of person – I like that no one gives Edie's performance a second look. She's seems to be having a good time and I don't think anyone would begrudge her that right now.

18

After the show, Edie is still buzzing with energy. It's hot and sticky in the Showbar after a few hours of lively singing and dancing and the crowd spills out onto the beach to get some air.

'Don't you want to stay behind to chat to your friend?' I ask. 'Which one was she? The front one, the fairy?'

Edie looks momentarily confused, but then she waves her hand, brushing the idea away. 'Oh, no. She'll be too busy, packing away and all that business. I'll see her another time. Let's get some air.'

We sit outside on the pebbles. Lots of the other people from the show seem to be doing the same thing. Some of them have brought their candles out with them, and there's a little campfire going down by the sea. One man has an acoustic guitar on his lap. The whole thing feels a bit like a mini festival.

'You don't need to get home, do you?' Edie asks. 'Your mum – will she worry?'

I laugh. 'I don't think my mother has ever been worried about me. I think I could be out for a fortnight and she still wouldn't wonder where I was.'

Edie looks at me carefully, then she smiles and rubs my arm. 'I'm sure that's not true. Silly!'

I don't say anything. Maybe it's not true. Maybe it is.

We sit in silence for a while, watching the waves lap the shore. Then Edie gets up suddenly. She goes over to the man with the acoustic guitar, a man with dreadlocks and a chunky red jumper. She leans down and says something to him and he grins. He passes her the guitar and gives her a thumbs up. She brings it back over to our little spot and sits down with her legs crossed, the guitar resting on one knee.

'Can you play it?' I ask.

Edie frowns in concentration for a moment.

'Well, it's been a while but . . .'

She plays a few duff notes but then she gets into her stride and strums a basic tune. Three notes in simple rhythm. Then she starts doing something intricate with the fingers on her right hand. It's nice. Peaceful.

'Sounds sort of Spanishy,' I say.

Edie grins and keeps playing. 'It's all coming back to me. Like riding a bike!' She stops and muffles the strings by placing her hands over them. She looks at me. 'Do you like music, Anna? Do you play any instruments?'

I shake my head.

Edie passes the guitar over to me and I take it uncertainly.

'Here,' she says, showing me. 'Rest it here. Hold this bit . . . here.' She scoots around the front of me and crouches down. She takes some of the fingers on my left hand and places them on certain strings.

'There. Now strum!'

I do as instructed. It makes a dull, thudding sound.

Edie laughs. 'Press harder with your left hand.'

I do as I'm told. 'It hurts! Feels like the strings are cutting my fingers.'

'You'll get used to it. Your fingers will get all tough on the ends. Try again.'

I strum again with my right hand; this time the sound rings out more clearly.

'There!' Edie says, sitting back on her heels and clapping her hands together. 'You just played an A minor!'

I grin back at her. 'Not sure you can play many songs with one chord though.'

'Maybe not,' she says. 'But you can play plenty with three.'

I smile and play my new A minor a few more times, each time sounding a little more springy than the last. Then I get up and take the guitar back to the guy in the red jumper. He thanks me and gives Edie a wave. She smiles back.

We look out at the sea again and I wonder if I should be getting home. But then I think, why? Mum won't care. All that'll happen when I get home is that I'll get into bed with my laptop and read junk on the internet until my eyes are sore and I fall asleep, and what's the point in that? Isn't *this* what we're supposed to do in life? Be in the great outdoors. Look at the sea. Meet new people. This is real life, the one that people are always going on about. I shouldn't be in a rush to get away from it, should I?

'You see there?' Edie points out to sea.

'The boats?' I can just about make out a few vessels, far out at sea, little circles of light bobbing around in the waves.

She nods. She brings her knees up to her chest and wraps her arms around them. 'You know when they go out to sea . . . far, far out to sea . . . did you know there's a big black curtain at the back there? When the boats get right up to the curtain, it opens up and lets the boats slip through. Into another world.'

I frown. I'm not sure what she's on about. 'You mean . . . to France?'

Edie shakes her head. 'No. Another world altogether. Another land . . . a different land . . .'

I don't say anything. I wonder how much Edie had to drink at the gig. And, again, I wonder if she is quite well in the head.

Then suddenly she shakes her head and laughs. 'Sorry,' she says. 'I haven't lost the plot, honest! That was just something my dad used to say to me. A silly story he'd tell me when I was little.'

'Oh, I see.' I laugh a bit too. Mostly out of relief.

'I always thought it'd be something I could carry on. Be one of those things I'd tell my own kids, but . . .' She shrugs and shakes her head again.

'You didn't want kids, then? With my dad, I mean?' It's a thought that's been running through my mind since I first met Edie, the idea that I might have some brothers and sisters knocking around somewhere. But if Edie has got kids she's been keeping them pretty quiet.

She shakes her head quickly and looks down, resting her chin on her knees again. 'We did talk about it. I always wanted them. My mum died when I was a baby so when I was growing up it was just me and my dad. He was great but it was always just the two of us. I'd go to friends' houses where there'd be lots of brothers and sisters and cousins and dogs all running around and I'd think, "Cor this is great. This is what I call a family!" and so I swore that I'd have lots of children, just as soon as I could. Hundreds of them, I thought! As many as I could fit in the house, and then some! Your dad, though . . . I don't know. There was a point, a few years ago, when it seemed like a possibility. It would come in little bursts – his sudden feeling that he wanted them. For a couple of weekends he'd seem keen, then something would come along at work and he'd seem to forget, or change his mind. It was funny things he'd get fixated on. One weekend we spent a whole day looking around kids' bed shops. He wanted to find a particular type of bed, he said – one of those high ones, a cabin bed, with a slide that kind of . . . curved down.' Edie makes a swooping gesture with her arm to illustrate. 'And it seemed strange to me at the time, that we were getting so hung up on this one thing – this one piece of furniture that would obviously be for a much older child – when I wasn't even pregnant yet.'

For one moment I wonder if maybe that bed had been for me. My dad had been trying to construct a bedroom for me, so I could come and stay. But then I realise I'm being ridiculous. He never even sent me a birthday card, for goodness' sake.

'But then he said something, something that made it all make sense. He said it was the type of bed he'd always dreamed of when he was a kid. And that's when it clocked with me. He didn't want a child. He wanted a child*hood*!' Edie laughs, a hard kind of laugh. 'He wanted to go back in time. He wasn't even ready to be a grown up, let alone a father.'

I get an image then, a memory, of my father bringing home a toy for me. It's one of those egg-timer shaped things that you juggle on a string. A Diablo, I think it was called. He demonstrated it a few times to me – spinning it quickly then throwing it up in the air and catching it on the string. He seemed delighted with it. After a few goes, he passed it to me. I went away and practised for hours, maybe even days. Eventually, I could throw it up and catch it on the string. I ran to find him. 'Look, Daddy!' I told him. 'I did it!'

'Hmm?' he says, barely looking. 'Yes. Very good.'

He'd lost interest. He'd had his go. He was never interested in whether I liked it really. He just wanted a new toy, an excuse to go to the toy shop. It makes sense now.

I realise that this is the first time I've heard Edie speak about James like this. She doesn't sound desperate any more. She doesn't even really sound sad. She sounds angry. I wonder if this is that stages of grief thing – she's in the angry stage right now; soon it will give way to confusion or acceptance or whatever comes next. Or, I think, maybe it's just that now he's been dead a few months she's ready to look back objectively at how he was. I suppose just because she's sad that he's dead, it doesn't mean that they always got on brilliantly. None of these thoughts are things I can say out loud.

The people sitting around us are starting to drift off home and I decide I should do the same. The autumn air is getting chilly. As I turn to tell Edie I need to be leaving, I see a familiar figure ambling towards us. He's wearing his long, woollen overcoat, his hair neatly combed as always.

'Oh, god,' I groan. 'It's Leon.'

19

Edie looks up and follows my gaze. 'Him *again*?' she whispers. Which is exactly what I'm thinking.

'Anna!' Leon calls cheerfully, as if he's forgotten how things ended the last time we spoke, how he hissed at me and threatened me. 'I thought it was you!'

'Hi,' I say. I'm not being particularly friendly, but then I don't want to be aggressive either. After our disastrous evening together I was angry, of course, but I was worried too. Had I blown it?

'I was just walking by. What on earth are you doing sitting out here with all these bizarre hippy types?' He looks around at the remains of the crowd. As his eyes fall on Edie, his lip curls slightly. I don't know if it's because he recognises her as the crying woman from the cafe, or just because she's dressed like a vampire. Either way, it annoys me.

I want to say something cutting, but I'm still too nervous. After our row the other night, I had worried the truth would be out. But so far, he doesn't seem to have said anything to anyone – my house hasn't been besieged by reporters or police – so there may still be a chance for me to win him back round, if I can bear to.

In the end I don't have to think up a suitable response because Leon doesn't bother to wait for an answer. 'I'm glad I've seen you, anyway,' he says. 'I've got something to show you and I think you're going to be *pretty* impressed . . .'

He reaches inside his satchel and takes out a magazine. I look at the front cover. It's called *Pencil* and it's apparently '*everything that's anything in the written word*'.

'Turn to page eighty-four,' he tells me.

It's an article – a story – entitled *The Witch's Hour*.

'Look, see there.' Leon jabs the page with his finger. 'What does it say?'

'*By Leon Jakes-Field*.' I look up at him. 'Brilliant,' I say with all the enthusiasm I can muster, which is not very much. 'Well done.'

Leon takes the magazine back from me and holds it out in front of him, looking over it proudly. 'I just found out myself last week,' he tells me. 'I'll never forget the moment when they called me. Hearing those words. "You're going to have your name in print." You know what the circulation is on this thing, Anna?'

I shake my head.

'Ten thousand. Ten thousand pairs of eyes on my work. Not bad, eh?'

'Nope. Not bad. Very good.'

'Anyway, I'll tell you what. You can keep that one,' he says, crouching down and pushing the copy towards me. 'Read the story, then let's chat! I'm interested in my readers' opinions, of course!'

He leans forward and pulls me into a horrible, weak hug. It almost makes me shiver. Then he turns, and with a kind of half salute, half wave, he strides away into the night.

I look down at the magazine in my hand and sigh. I'm suddenly hit by the terrible, never-endingness of it all. We could be at the same school for another three years if we both stay on for sixth form. And then what, after that? When we go to university or get jobs or whatever, will he still want to 'spend time with me'? Will I be forced to do what he says, when he says, for ever? Never able to tell him what I think of him, never able to explain to anyone why I can't get rid of him?

I notice that Edie is looking at me strangely. 'Are you OK?'

'What? Yeah.'

'You don't like that boy very much, do you?'

There's no point lying. Edie doesn't really count anyway. 'Not really.'

'He doesn't seem very likable.'

'No.'

'Begs the question, then: why don't you tell him to sling his hook?'

I just shake my head and look down at the magazine in my hands again. 'I've got to go,' I tell her, getting to my feet.

'No.' She grabs my wrist. 'Wait. Stay for a minute.'

I'm slightly taken aback. I sit back down. 'Why?'

'You're uncomfortable. It's something to do with that boy. It's upsetting you. I can see it. What is it? What's he making you do?'

'Oh, nothing. He's not making me do anything. Not really.'

'What is it, then? You can't really be that meek and mild, can you? You strike me as the kind of girl to give a bloke a black eye if he wound you up too much.' She gives me a playful punch on the arm. 'So is he blackmailing you or what?'

106

Edie is joking, and I've never really considered the term blackmail before, but now she's said it, I realise she's right. He's not demanding money but he is demanding me. My time. My company. He *is* blackmailing me. How did I not realise this before?

Edie's face has changed. She's not grinning any more. 'What? Good god, he is blackmailing you, isn't he? Anna, what's he got on you? What is it? I'm sure there must be something we can do?'

And I don't know what it is – maybe it's the candles or the sea, or maybe it's just because now I have a name for it. Blackmail. I'm being blackmailed. Yes, I did something wrong, but blackmail is wrong too, isn't it? I decide I do want to tell someone, to let them know exactly what Leon is like. And Edie, this strange woman sitting here with me in her Dracula cloak, she seems just separate enough from the rest of my life, from the real world, to seem like the perfect confidante.

So I tell her the whole thing.

20

It was last May. A few weeks earlier I'd stopped working with Martina at The Last Drop, partly because I really needed to put some more time into my coursework but also because Martina's shouting and unrelenting efficiency-drives were starting to do my head in. I hadn't put much money aside while I was working though, so I was finding the sudden drop in income difficult. I was considering just biting the bullet and asking Martina for my job back, but I wasn't even sure if she'd have me. What I really wanted was something more casual, a way to make a bit of pocket money when I needed to, without committing myself to a full day a week somewhere. It was George who suggested the idea.

'Babysitting,' he said. 'Easiest way to make fast money. I do it myself sometimes, if I need a quick cash injection into the business.'

'For what kids, though? I don't know any.'

'Kids are everywhere.' He gestured around him vaguely. 'This town can't move for all the kids. Put a card up in the newsagent.'

'Do people really do that in real life? Isn't that what the internet's for?'

George sat up and looked at me. 'Anna. Promise me that whatever you do, you will not advertise for children on the internet. It's not a good look.'

I laughed. 'Fair point.'

So I did exactly as George suggested. I wrote a short advert on a small piece of card and asked Miserable Karen in the paper shop if I could stick it up in the window. When I went in a few days later, Miserable Karen told me that a local man had been asking about the advert. 'He wanted to know what you were like – if you were to be trusted and all that.'

'Oh, right. What did you tell him?'

Karen seemed surprised by the question. 'Well, I said I didn't know. I don't know anything about you, do I? You come in here for your crisps and drinks but I don't know if you can be trusted. But I told him you've never nicked anything, and you seem quite normal enough to me.'

'OK. Thanks.'

I was pretty sure that after Karen's less-than-glowing reference, I wouldn't hear anything else, but a day or two later I answered my phone to a well-spoken man who said, 'Um. Hello . . . Are you Anna? The babysitter?'

I found it quite funny, the idea that 'babysitter' was somehow now my identity, or even my job description, on the strength of one card in the paper shop window. My only babysitting experience up until this point had been looking after George's little sisters. But I went along with it anyway.

The man's name was Gerrard Bradstock and he had a six-year-old son called Shay. He told me that his wife had just left him – 'for her dental hygienist. And she hasn't even got nice teeth!' – and that he was having difficulty finding childcare for Shay on Tuesday evenings when he had to be out for a few hours to attend a meeting for some charity committee he was on. He gave me a light grilling on who I was and my experience with children and I gave him a slightly exaggerated summary of the times I'd looked after the twins, but I don't know how much he really listened. I got the feeling he was a little bit desperate and keen to get this arrangement tied down as quickly as possible.

The following Tuesday I arrived at the Bradstocks' house, ready to meet my charge. The house was in a nice part of town, on a tree-lined road where all of the houses looked like enormous country mansions. Gerrard was exactly as I imagined him from our phone call – smartly turned out, neatly combed hair, tailored clothes. He looked tired though, under his polished finish. He had bags under his eyes and he was too thin. He seemed highly strung. Stressed. I assumed that this was probably on account of his marriage problems. But then I met Shay.

The kid was a little nightmare.

I'd thought my brief was simple – I had to entertain him an hour, feed him his tea, then entertain him for another hour. My first clue that he might be a bit on the difficult side came when Gerrard's parting words to me were, 'Really he should be in bed before I get home, but there's no way you'll be able to manage that, so just . . . do whatever you can with him.'

When Gerrard had left, I thought I should probably say hello to the kid, introduce myself, so I went over to where he was sitting, cross-legged, right up at the television screen.

'Hi, Shay. I'm Anna. How are you?'

Shay kept his eyes on the telly. 'Piss off.'

I was shocked. This kid was six – the same age as George's sisters. The idea of the twins coming out with something like that was unimaginable. But as it turned out, a bit of swearing was the least of my worries. As soon as his cartoon was over, he began systematically destroying the house.

He ripped stuffing out of cushions, he drew on the wallpaper with felt-tip pens, he knocked over chairs. He threw two plates from the top of the stairs, showering the hallway – and me – with shards of porcelain.

Obviously I told him to stop. I tried everything. Being firm and reasonable, screaming and shouting. Pleading and begging. But Shay just acted as if I wasn't there at all. I tried to call Gerrard – to tell him this wasn't what I'd signed up for – but his phone was switched off. At one point, after nearly forty-five minutes of destruction, I swear I actually contemplated calling the police.

But then, all of a sudden, Shay seemed to lose interest in his campaign of terror. He walked calmly into the lounge, turned the television right up, and parked himself in front of it. He stayed like that for nearly an hour. I kept looking around at the balls of cushion stuffing, the piles of soil from the house plants, the smashed glass, wondering if I should make an effort to tidy up, but I didn't dare move in case it stirred Shay from his trance and he kicked off again.

When Gerrard returned that night, I expected him to be horrified by the state of the house but he barely raised an eyebrow. Evidently this kind of scene was par for the course in the Bradstock house. It also explained why Gerrard had been so happy to hand Shay over to an inexperienced teenager he'd found in a newsagent's window – clearly no one else would have him.

As I walked home that night, I decided that that would be the last I would see of lovely little Shay. No amount of money was worth going through that hell again and, anyway, I was pretty sure there were plenty of other, non-demonic children I could babysit for instead. I knew that week I'd have to phone Gerrard to let him know I wouldn't be coming the following Tuesday, or, in fact, ever again, but I kept putting the phone call off. I knew I'd be dropping him in it – I had a feeling that people wouldn't exactly be queuing up to take over my role. Then, on the Saturday night, he called me.

He was really sorry to ask but could I watch Shay for one hour, two hours max, on Sunday afternoon. He had an aunt who was in hospital and he had to go and sit with her while she had some tests or other. He'd pay me double, 'for the short notice'. I wanted to say no, of course. I wanted to think of any excuse to get out of it, but what can I say? I'm a coward. I don't like saying no to people. I hate to let people down. So I reasoned that the money would certainly be helpful so I said yes. I promised I'd be there at two o'clock sharp the next day.

And dear god is that a promise I've regretted ever since.

21

The following afternoon, when the sun was high and it was about a hundred degrees in the shade, I arrived at the Bradstocks' once again. This time, I was relieved to see that Shay was in the garden – I figured he'd be slightly easier to manage out there, where there wasn't quite as much to smash or tear apart. He seemed to be engrossed in some kind of digging activity over by the fence.

'He's just doing some weeding,' Gerrard told me with an exhausted smile.

We looked over at Shay who was pulling up clumps of flowers by the handful and tossing them behind him onto the lawn.

Gerrard left, and this time I decided not to risk approaching Shay. Instead, I sat down on the step at the edge of the patio and watched him from a safe distance. I suppose the truth was, I was hoping he wouldn't notice me at all. I wanted to get through the next hour or two with as little interaction with him as possible.

'He's a delightful boy, isn't he?'

I recognised the voice but I couldn't quite place it so I turned around and saw Leon, sitting in a chair in the garden next door. It wasn't a deck chair; it was an armchair. A proper leather armchair. He'd obviously dragged it outside. I guess a collapsible canvas deck chair wasn't good enough for someone of Leon's talent and importance. He had his legs crossed, a notepad resting in his lap.

'What are you doing here?' I said, without much effort to be friendly or polite. This was before the whole thing had happened, of course, so there was no need for me to pretend to Leon that I liked him.

'I live here,' he said simply.

I supposed that made sense. This was just about the poshest road in town and it was well-known that Leon's family was loaded since his mum had signed her film deal.

I didn't bother replying. I just went back to watching Shay, who by now seemed to be getting bored of his weeding. He threw a few handfuls of soil around the lawn in a lacklustre kind of way, then stood up and came over to where I was sitting. He stood looking at me for a while. He didn't say anything; he just stared, his dark eyes staring me right in the face. It was quite unnerving.

Then a noise at the back of the garden disturbed him. He spun around. We both watched a cat jump down from the wall and stalk across the back of the garden.

Shay suddenly let out a sharp hiss, but the cat was too far away to hear, so he stopped hissing and shouted, 'Piss off, cat!'

'Don't say piss, Shay,' I said, slightly nervously.

Shay kept his eyes on the cat, watching it as it roamed around the lawn at the end of the garden. 'My mum says that all cats should be chopped up and put in curry.'

'Your mum sounds like a lovely woman,' I replied.

'My mum is a pirate and she's in a boat at the moment. Finding treasure for me.'

'Is that right?' I said flatly. I wasn't surprised that no one had wanted to fill Shay in on the truth about Mummy's new lover, the dental hygienist.

'Yes.' Shay was looking at me again now. 'And then she's going to come back and kill all the cats and put them in curry. And then she's going to kill you and put you in curry.'

With this, Shay darted off across the garden in pursuit of the cat. The cat was too busy licking its paws to see Shay coming, so was taken completely by surprise when Shay launched himself into the air, and landed right on top of it. The cat squealed. Shay screamed in delight. I realised I had to do something.

I stood up. 'Shay!' I shouted. 'Get off him now!'

Shay just laughed again, the cat still pinned under his body, desperately trying to wriggle free. Shay began a chant: 'Cat curry, cat curry, cat curry, cat curry!'

Next door, Leon was now on his feet standing at the fence between the two gardens. 'Can't you keep the odious little thing quiet? I came out here to work.'

I ignored him, his work not exactly being my main priority at that moment.

I realised Shay wasn't going to be put off with a verbal warning, so I jogged over to him, grabbed him by both shoulders and tried to wrestle him free of the cat. Shay wasn't ready to come without a struggle though. He just gripped the cat tighter and chanted faster. 'Cat curry, cat curry, cat curry, cat curry.'

I moved my grip downwards until I had Shay in a kind of rugby tackle, his arms pinned at his sides. The cat was able to leap free, letting out a final screech and diving for the cover of the hedge. I wasn't sure how good cats' memories were but I sincerely hoped it remembered not to take a short cut across this garden again.

Shay was furious at my interception. He turned on me, pummelling my stomach with his fists and kicking me in the shins.

'Stop it!' I shouted. 'Get off me, you little bastard!'

Shay's response was to grab hold of my arm, bring my wrist up to his mouth and sink his teeth hard into the skin. The next bit is a blur of pain and anger, but I know I screamed and pulled my arm away, and then I pushed him. One quick shove in the middle of his chest.

Shay let out a cry – but I'm sure it was just out of frustration. The push knocked him off balance and he toppled backwards, tripping over a flowerpot on his way. Then, I still don't know why or how – I really don't think the shove was that hard – but he fell, hitting the back of his head on the hard edge of the patio. I waited for him to get back up, to swear or shout or carry on attacking me but he didn't.

He just lay there.

Completely still.

22

'Shay?' I looked down at him. 'Shay?'

'Good god, Anna. You've knocked out a six-year-old.'

I'd forgotten about Leon, still standing at the fence, looking over at us, an amused sneer on his face.

'Shut up,' I hissed at him.

But then Shay opened his eyes and blinked slowly. I heard myself sigh with relief.

'Shay?' I said again. 'Are you OK?'

Shay didn't respond at first. He just blinked once more. Then he twisted his face into his usual scowl and pushed himself up to a sitting position, his eyes locked on me the whole time.

I was frozen, kneeling by the step, looking right back at him. He clambered to his feet without taking his eyes off me and began backing slowly away to the far end of the garden. It was then that I realised: he was scared. Scared of me.

'Shay . . .' I started again, but the sound of my voice made him flinch. He turned and darted off to the end of the garden, where he crouched behind a camellia bush and peered out at me, like a small animal hiding from a predator.

The sound of clapping made me jump. Loud, slow claps.

'Well done,' Leon said, still smirking. 'Quite a display. You've terrified a small child. How proud you must feel.'

I didn't reply. I just looked at Leon, my mouth slightly open. I felt dazed. Then I looked back at Shay, crouching in the corner.

Leon started to laugh then, shaking his head, his hands in his pockets, like an indulgent old uncle.

'Shut up,' I muttered. 'Shut *up*.'

Leon didn't say anything. He just sat back down in his leather armchair and continued to survey the scene.

I decided to ignore him completely. I perched on the edge of the patio, breathing hard. What was going to happen when Gerrard got home? Should I tell him what had happened? How would I explain it? He knew Shay was a handful but he was six years old, for god's sake, there was really no excuse for me smashing his head on a paving slab, was there? But then there was Shay himself. What would he say? And would Gerrard believe him? Unless – it suddenly occurred to me – unless there was evidence. An injury. At this point I realised that regardless of the evidential value of an injury, I should really check Shay's head. What if he was bleeding to death over there?

I stood up and walked slowly towards him. 'Shay . . .' I said, being careful to keep my voice soft and unthreatening, 'Shay, I just need to have a look –'

'No!' he shouted, and retreated further under the camellia bush. 'Don't touch me!'

'I'm not going to . . . I just need to . . .' As I got closer, I realised there was indeed a dark smudge on Shay's collar – I still don't know to this day if it was blood, or if it was, whether it was a result of my push, because Shay didn't let me get any closer.

He shouted 'No!' again in such a high-pitched, panicked voice that I had no choice but to back off. I retreated to my spot at the edge of the patio and sat there for the next hour. Neither Shay nor I moved in that time. We stayed rooted to our camps in opposite corners of the garden.

I didn't know what was going to happen when Gerrard got home. My mind darted around from one scenario to the next – I'd just tell Gerrard exactly what had happened. He knew what Shay was like, he wouldn't be that angry, he might even apologise for his behaviour. But then I realised I was kidding myself. Parental instincts are strong. If Gerrard found out that I'd physically assaulted Shay – that his head had smashed into a paving stone – he'd be furious. Would he even call the police, I thought with a sudden cold flush of panic.

I was no closer to reaching a decision on the right thing to do when Gerrard finally arrived home. I didn't hear his car pull into the drive so it made me jump when he stepped out of the back door to join us in the garden.

'Hi there,' he called. 'How's he been?'

He looked nervously towards the end of the garden. By this point, although still squatting in the camellia bush, Shay no longer looked so much like a frightened mouse. He was sitting cross-legged, poking his fingers into the soil.

'Uh, yeah,' I said, standing up slowly. 'OK.' I looked over the fence but Leon was nowhere to be seen. I don't know when he'd left.

'Yeah?' Gerrard said. He seemed surprised that I didn't have any complaints to file, any catastrophes to report.

'Yeah,' I said again. 'Fine.'

I wasn't consciously not telling him – I just couldn't find the words. I couldn't think where to begin.

Just then, Shay came pelting out of the bushes. He sprinted across the lawn and threw himself at Gerrard. He clung to him, his arms wrapped tightly around his waist.

I just stood there, frozen, looking at them both – Shay's face buried in Gerrard's stomach, Gerrard looking down at Shay, bemused. I was waiting for Shay to say something – 'Get her away from me', 'She hit me' – that kind of thing. But he didn't.

'Hi there, Shay,' Gerrard said, chuckling uncertainly. 'You OK there, pal?'

Shay didn't say anything. He just held on tighter.

Gerrard looked up at me. 'I guess he missed me!' he laughed, shaking his head, obviously baffled by this uncharacteristic display of affection.

'I guess.' I looked down at the ground, poking a tuft of grass with my toe.

Then Shay wriggled himself away from Gerrard, jogged back over to the end of the garden and started bouncing a football against the wall.

'You're obviously doing something right!' Gerrard said, with a shrug and a tired smile.

I didn't say anything. But what could I have said? 'Actually, I beat him up. That's what did the trick'?

I didn't know if Shay would tell Gerrard what happened later. I didn't know if Leon would tell him. I didn't know if Gerrard would believe either of them in any event. I just knew I wanted to get out of that garden as quickly as possible.

'I better get going then . . .' I picked up my bag and headed for the side gate, but Gerrard called me back.

'Anna, your money.'

I stopped and waited as he pulled his wallet out of his back pocket and took out two ten-pound notes. Then, after a pause, he added an extra five. 'As you . . . you know. As he seems so happy.'

I felt awful. Accepting payment for roughing up his kid, like a gangster. But I knew it would look weird if I refused it so I just stuffed the cash into the front pocket of my rucksack, put my head down and made for the gate.

It was as I stepped onto the pavement and clicked the gate closed behind me that I heard his voice. 'Decided not to mention your little . . . contretemps, then?'

Leon was leaning against the wall at the front of his house, his hands in his pockets, his legs casually crossed. He was still wearing his expression, that amused sneer, head on one side.

I didn't say anything. I just stared at him.

'I mean, he's probably going to be OK, isn't he? Even if Shay does squeal about his nasty babysitter attacking him, who's going to believe him?'

Leon pushed himself off the wall and casually walked towards me. When he eventually stopped he was just that bit too close to me. I took a step backwards, but he came closer again.

'I mean, it'll be his word against yours, won't it? It's not as if there's any . . . evidence.'

I realised then he was holding something up, right in my face. It was his phone. I squinted at it, trying to get it into focus.

I saw then that there was a video on screen. He was showing me a clip of something.

It was a clip of me.

There I was, just an hour earlier, calling Shay's name, and there was Shay, crouching under the camellia bush. I approached him; he recoiled, terrified. Then the video cut to me shouting at Shay – when I was telling him to get off the cat – but you couldn't see the cat or Shay in the video. Just me shouting, storming towards Shay. Then it cut to me rugby tackling him, then our tussle – although no sign of the bite. It just jumped straight to me pushing him, flinging him into the patio. A final shot of Shay's face, eyes closed, motionless, that dark smudge on his collar, clearly visible and decidedly blood-like. It was all there. All the action. When had he started filming me?

'You . . . changed it,' I said quietly.

I mean, I did know it was a bad run of events anyway, but Leon had made it worse. The way he'd put the scene of me approaching Shay first and him cowering under the bush – as if I'd been pursuing him all day, tormenting him. The way he'd cut out the vicious bite, so it looked like I'd just pushed Shay totally unprovoked, in an act of uncontrolled rage.

Leon slipped the phone back into his pocket. 'I think I captured the most critical elements, don't you?'

I didn't reply.

Then I realised I was crying, but I don't remember feeling very much. Just dizzy and numb and very, very tired. Suddenly Leon was right in front of me. He reached up towards my face, and brushed away a tear with his thumb.

'Oh, Anna,' he said in that light, amused voice he loves to use so much. 'Funny little Anna. You don't need to worry. I'm not going to tell anyone. Lovely Shay was running, he tripped, he fell, he hit his head. Children are always hitting their heads, especially little hooligans like Shay. No one will ever know what really happened. It'll be our secret. Yours,' he takes my hand, and clasps it between both of his, 'and mine.'

I was too stunned to know what to make of it all. I just stood there, my hand resting cold and limp in Leon's.

'Now,' he said, putting one hand on my back as if to help me up. 'I think you should probably get out of here, don't you?'

I didn't know if that's what I *should* do, but it was very much what I wanted to do. I didn't say anything else. I just turned and ran. I kept running until I was almost home.

23

Edie looks at me carefully. 'So did the boy tell his father? Did Leon tell him?'

I shake my head. 'No. Not yet, anyway.'

'Well, maybe you should just go over there – tell the boy's father. Tell Gerrard. Then it's out, it's done. Leon can't do anything else.'

Obviously this is a solution I've been over a hundred times. And actually, the day after it all happened, I was fully prepared to do it.

I'd lain awake all night thinking about it. It had been an accident. I'd just been trying to stop Shay killing that cat. And then he'd bitten me. It'd been self-defence. And cat defence. It was excusable. No lasting damage had been done. I should go and tell Gerrard the full story before Leon had a chance to show them his horrible doctored video. But that morning, when I booted up my computer, I found an email from Leon. There was no text, no covering note. Just three links to websites, a photo and some pasted paragraphs.

The photo was of Shay – a still from the video. Shay, lying on the ground, eyes closed. It was chilling, shown like that, it really was. Out of context. When you couldn't see it was only a few seconds till he opened his eyes.

The paragraphs pasted below had been copied from somewhere else on the internet. They were written in a small, dense font.

The first one said:

Children Act 2004, section 58

Battery of a child causing actual bodily harm to the child cannot be justified on the ground that it constituted reasonable punishment.

And just below, this:

Offences Against the Person Act 1861, section 47

Whosoever shall be convicted upon an indictment of any assault occasioning actual bodily harm shall be liable for a term not exceeding 7 years.

Seven years. I felt my stomach flip.

I clicked on the first link. It was to a news article about a babysitter found guilty of assault and imprisoned for five years. The authorities had found 'more than 40 bruises' on the four-year-old girl's body. The babysitter had protested her innocence, claiming that she was just trying to stop the girl fighting with her sister.

The other two stories were similar. The assaults were all

worse than what I'd done to Shay – I felt sure of that, even though I knew I'd hurt him. One child had bite marks down his arms. Another had scald marks where a full cup of coffee had been poured over his legs – but although I knew these stories were more extreme, I could see what they all had in common: all the babysitters had blamed the child – for being noisy or difficult, for being so rough that they had to be restrained – but all had ended up with prison time anyway.

I'd slammed my laptop shut. Then I'd got into bed, pulled a pillow over my head, and vowed I'd do whatever it took to keep Leon quiet.

I tell Edie about the email now – about the news stories, about the legal passages. She chews her lip anxiously. 'Are you sure? Seven seems a lot, doesn't it? A lot of years. Are you sure that's quite right?'

I nod slowly. 'I think so. I looked it up myself. Searched and searched, read loads of legal pages. I hoped Leon was just messing with me. But it looks right. And actual bodily harm is anything, really! Like, even a scratch or a bruise.' I pause. Edie doesn't say anything. She looks uncomfortable. 'But even without that,' I go on, 'even without the laws and the actual bodily harm – what would people think? If they saw that video? If Leon puts it . . . puts it anywhere, it will be around school, around town – around the world! – just like that. In a flash. Everyone will know. Everyone will hate me. That will be my reputation for ever.' I bury my face in my hands. 'It's all such a mess.'

Edie rubs my back. 'Hey, come on, now. It's not that bad. It's not that bad.'

126

I don't say anything but we both know reassurance is kind of meaningless. We're quiet again, for a long time this time. Five, maybe ten minutes.

'Hey, you know what, I was going to say something earlier.' I can tell by her change in tone she's going to change the subject and I'm glad. 'I was going to tell you this idea I had.'

'Yeah?'

'Yeah. I was going to say, I've been thinking. About living down here, on the coast.'

'You mean moving?'

Edie shrugs. 'Yeah. I mean, it seems like time for a change. I feel like I'm "at a crossroads" as they say. And I do like to be beside the seaside!'

'Do you know anyone down here?'

'I know you!' she says with a nervous laugh.

I'm not sure what to say to that so I don't say anything. Edie stops laughing and looks embarrassed. 'I'm joking, obviously, I mean . . .'

She trails off and it's awkward for a moment. Then I'm just thinking that it's not as if she's got a job she'd have to leave, so she might as well go wherever she likes, when I remember about the CVs, still sitting in my bag.

'Oh god, I nearly forgot!' I take them out and pass them to her.

'Oh!' she says, taking them. 'My CV! Me too!'

She peers at them closely, tilting them to try to get them in the light of nearby bars. Then she runs her hand over the paper, stroking them like they're something rare and beautiful. 'Oh, Anna,' she says quietly. 'Look at this. Would you *look* at this . . .' She's quiet again while she reads it through. I feel embarrassed suddenly. I wonder if I've taken a bit of a liberty, embellishing it like that. She only asked me to type the thing up, after all. Who do I think I am?

Edie laughs suddenly and claps her hands together. 'Look at this! Look at this bit! *"Took full responsibility for visual merchandising and displays"* – how grand am I!' She laughs again and shakes her head. 'I don't even know what those words mean!'

'I just thought you weren't making the most of things. You know – your experience and all that. I hope you don't mind.'

Edie turns to look at me, her eyes shining. 'I love it! I love it! I tell you what, Anna, I'm going to be able to get me any job I want with these little beauties!' She holds the wodge of paper in the air and shakes it triumphantly. 'I'm going to move down to the coast, get me a little flat – nothing special, but nice enough – then I'll find a job, in a tourist shop or what have you, and then it'll all be OK! It's all going to be OK!'

She seems so completely delighted it's hard not to feel a bit emotional. Although in the short time I've known Edie I've gathered that she's a put-a-brave-face-on-it kind of woman, she's always had a sadness about her, even when she's cracking jokes or chattering on about nothing. I guess it's to be expected, what with everything she's been through. There's something about her eyes, I think, or the way her smile fades as soon as she stops talking. But now, sitting here in the moonlight, her velvet cape wrapped around her knees, I think she might be really, genuinely happy.

24

Edie doesn't waste any time getting started on her plans for a new life. The week after our Halloween gig and our evening on the beach, she rings me.

'Anna, I've lined up five – no, *six*! – flats to look at on Saturday. Six! Are you free? Do you think you'd come with me? I need a second pair of eyes and it'd be so helpful to have someone who knows the area. Last thing I want is to end up moving right into the middle of a crime hotspot or something!'

This time, I'm not surprised to hear from Edie and I'm not surprised by her invitation. When we finally left the beach to head home that night after the gig, I had no doubt that I'd see her again. It wasn't just because she'd decided to move down here and it wasn't even because of my confession. I think the truth was, I realised I just really like her. I enjoy her company. It's different being with her to being with George and Sienna or anyone else from school. And it's a *lot* different to being with Mum. I like who I am with her. I feel like I make a difference to her life. Like she likes having me around.

Also, by now I've got the impression that Edie doesn't really have a lot of people in her life. From the way she talks about

129

the last few years – not to mention the state of her CV – I get the feeling she basically devoted every last ounce of her time and energy to my father. Personally I think that was a kind of ridiculous thing to do and I'm guessing now that he's dropped dead and left her with nothing she's starting to think so too, but still. We are where we are.

Another thing I'm noticing is that there's something childlike about Edie. There just seems to be so much stuff she doesn't know about, things that she finds amazing. I have a pretty good idea that this is the main reason she's still seeking me out, treating me like a friend.

I think at first it was all about the connection to my dad – I don't know, maybe it's comforting, me being evidence that he existed or something – but now I really think the main reason Edie keeps calling and texting is because at fifteen years old, I'm kind of in the same place as she is, mentally speaking. She doesn't really strike me as a true adult at all. I can't really imagine her sitting down at a dinner party with the kind of people my mum has over, for example. She'd be totally panicked.

'Uh, yeah. I can look at flats with you, no problem. Where are they all?'

Edie reels off a list of road names – some I've heard of, some I haven't. I give her a quick overview of the areas I know and we agree to meet at the weekend, outside the first flat on her list.

The evening before I'm due to meet Edie, I'm at Sienna's, sitting beside her on her bed while she reads me weird news stories off the internet.

'Ew, listen to this: "*I kept biscuits in my fat folds*. Tina, forty-eight, claims she was so desperate to hide her overeating from her children that she'd store custard creams in the crevices between her own folds of flesh." That is so repugnant.'

I make a face, and Sienna lifts her top and looks down at her own stomach. She grips an inch of skin between her thumb and forefinger. 'Tell me honestly. Am I fat? Am I custard-cream Tina?'

I give her the briefest of glances. 'Don't be a twat, Sienna.'

She pulls her T-shirt back over her stomach. 'We have to go spinning. You promised.'

'Remind me again – what's spinning?'

'Exercise bikes. Super, super fast.' She makes the cycling motion with her arms.

I groan. 'Oh, god. Not that.'

'You *promised*. I came to that weird comic fest thing with you on the condition you'd come spinning with me.'

She's right. I don't say anything.

'It's tomorrow morning. I'll pick you up at eleven.'

I'm meeting Edie at ten to twelve tomorrow. 'Can't we do it on Sunday? Or after school or something?'

'No. Saturday morning is when the class is.'

'Well . . . I'm busy.'

'Doing what?'

'Stuff. Homework. Just stuff I've got to do.'

Sienna looks at me through narrowed eyes. 'You're lying. Why are you lying?'

'I'm not!' I protest, but I know my cheeks are flushed. I'm not much good at lying.

131

Sienna just looks at me, waiting for me to crumble. Which I do after about thirty seconds. 'I'm helping Edie look at flats.'

I know Sienna will find this weird but what I don't realise is how much it will annoy her.

'Anna!' She hits me with a pillow. 'For god's sake! Not her *again*? And what do you mean, "look at flats"? Oh, please god tell me she's not *moving* here?'

I just shrug and go back to flicking through my magazine. I'm not going to rise to Sienna. I'm not going to let her make this into a bigger deal than it is.

Sienna isn't ready to let it go though. She turns to face me, her legs crossed in front of her. 'Anna, seriously. Look at me. Don't you think it's weird? Come on. You must. I think she's stalking you.'

'Don't be a twat, Sienna.'

'Anna, she's like, fifty years old and she wants to spend all her time with a teenager. It's tragic. George told me when he saw you with her on the pier that time that she was dressed like a kids' TV presenter on acid and when he turned up she legged it without even saying bye. It's all weird. She's making *you* weird. What is it about her? Are you looking for a new mum or what?'

She's really pissing me off now. She can be so black and white sometimes. So judgemental. I just feel like they're totally different parts of my life, different worlds. There's George and Sienna and school and the normal stuff in one part, then Edie and playing the guitar and going to underground gigs in another part. I don't even want Sienna to comment on Edie. She knows nothing about her. She should mind her own business.

It's my turn to spin around now, to look at Sienna and face her head-on. 'OK, so firstly, she's not fifty. She's like, forty. Not even that, probably. And secondly, you think *everything* is weird, Sienna. Anything. You're so smug sometimes, you *and* George. You think you're so cool and quirky and intelligent and amazing and that everyone else is a weirdo or a try-hard or a loser. Seriously. You and George are not the only OK people on the planet, you know!'

I'm on my feet now although I don't know when it happened.

Sienna doesn't look shocked or offended or even mildly irritated. She's still just looking at me, regarding me coolly. She waits for me to finish shouting. Then she just puts her head on one side and looks at me for a moment. 'I think you've proved my point, don't you?' She looks back at her laptop screen as if to tell me the conversation is over. She always has to have the last word.

I leave her room, slamming her bedroom door behind me. On my way home I make a silent resolution not to talk to George or Sienna about Edie ever again. If I'm seeing her, I'll make up an excuse. If she calls, I'll say it was someone else.

They'll both assume she's long gone.

25

When Edie and I meet the following day, she's full of nervous energy. The first flat is in Newton Road, in the east of town. It's not quite the crime hotspot she was worried about but it's not exactly the nicest area either. The houses are identical terraces packed in tight and there are rusty bikes, discarded sofas and washing machines scattered up and down the pavements.

'Nice quiet road!' Edie comments brightly, looking house number eight up and down, where we're due to look at the flat on the lower ground floor.

The agent arrives and shakes Edie's hand, and then mine too. I can see him wondering what the set-up is – if I'm her daughter or what – but it's not really something anyone's got the time to go into.

The agent does his best with his spiel – compact, central, convenient, all the rest – but the fact is, the flat is a dive. It smells like mould and stale cigarette smoke. The carpet is curling up at the edges. The kitchen is tiny: one hob ring and a sink.

Edie looks at it doubtfully. 'I do so love a bit of cooking though . . .'

'It's only the first one,' I say to her as we leave. 'The next one will be better.'

But it's not. Not really. I can't claim to know much about the rental market in my home town but I'm quickly realising one thing: Edie's budget won't get her very much.

Even the agent seems a bit uncomfortable. I guess it can't be much fun trying to pretend that these rotten little flea pits could be a 'cosy new home' and as the day wears on I notice his enthusiasm gradually wane. But then, late in the afternoon when the light is fading and I'm honestly about ready to give up, he gets a phone call from his office. He steps away from us to take it and when he comes back over, he seems brighter.

'We've had something new come on. It's a bit of an unusual set-up, but it's definitely worth a look.'

I don't hold out much hope as I'm pretty sure 'unusual' is estate agent speak for 'totally awful and bizarre' but as we walk to Denmark Run – a row of brightly coloured houses set back from the seafront – the agent explains that the woman who owns the place has moved to Dubai for three years and her main priority is that her flat is taken care of properly.

'She's willing to offer a heavily discounted rate if a tenant can take on a certain amount of maintenance – the odd bit of decorating, basic repairs, keeping the garden flourishing . . . that kind of thing.'

Edie turns to me, eyes shining. 'A garden!'

The flat is actually beautiful. You can see why the owner doesn't want just any old person to move in and start spilling things on the plush cream carpet or burning cigarette holes in the heavy silk curtains. The main room – an all-in-one kitchen

135

and living room – is light and airy with a floor to ceiling window running along the whole front wall. The kitchen in the corner is small but seems to have everything you'd need and the worktops and cupboard doors are all sparkling and new.

'And the really interesting thing about it is, it's sort of a two-bedroom place,' the agent says as he guides us around.

'Sort of?' I ask.

'Yeah.' The agent signals for us to follow him and he crosses the hall to a door at the back. 'We're not allowed to officially advertise it as two-bed, because it hasn't got a proper window, but it's still a good space.'

He pushes the door open and we can see that the room is indeed a good space. It's not massive, but it's plenty big enough for a bed and it even has a little en suite bathroom. As he says, it doesn't have a proper full-size window, but it does have a little strip of glass running along the top of the wall just below the ceiling. I recognise the type of window from the changing rooms at school – it's just enough to give a bit of ventilation and light.

'It backs out onto the garden.' The agent gestures to the little window. 'I suppose it was originally some kind of outdoor storage space.'

'Wow-*ee*,' Edie says, gazing around as if she's being shown the Royal Suite at The Savoy. 'What a wonderful bonus.'

'Yes, exactly,' the agent says, nodding enthusiastically. 'A bonus.'

Edie sweeps around the flat, running her hand along the gleaming woodwork and pristine work surfaces. Then she stands in the middle of the huge lounge and spins around and around, her arms outstretched. I'm worried the agent might think she's a bit mad and so not to be trusted with this nice flat, but he just chuckles and says, 'You'll take it, then?'

She stops spinning and looks at him, wide-eyed. 'Oh yes, yes, yes! If I'm allowed?'

She sounds so much like a kid who's been told they're going to Disneyworld that I have to try really hard not to laugh.

The agent shrugs. 'Sure. The owner particularly wanted a single person, actually – didn't want kids rubbing their grubby fingers on the walls. You haven't got pets, have you?'

Edie shakes her head earnestly. 'Oh, no. Not me, sir.'

'Excellent, excellent,' the agent says, opening the front door. 'In that case, let's get back to the office and get the paperwork done.'

Edie claps her hands together. As we follow the agent outside, she gives me a wink.

Exactly one week later, Edie and I are standing back in the airy flat on Denmark Run, surrounded by Edie's boxes and suitcases that a gruff man called Neil has unloaded from his grubby transit van for the bargain price of fifty quid, cash in hand.

'I live here!' Edie tells me. 'I live here!' She looks around at the bags and boxes on the floor. 'I don't even know where to start. I suppose – with the essentials?'

I nod. 'Yes. Probably best.'

It's quite slow going as Edie keeps getting distracted by arranging her bathroom shelves so the prettiest bottles are at the front and choosing which duvet cover best matches the wallpaper in the bedroom, but in just over three hours we manage to unpack everything. As we work, I realise I'm subconsciously on the lookout for clues about what Edie's life with my father was like.

Edie doesn't have many photos in frames. There are three albums, but I don't feel I can exactly start rifling through them. I don't find anything obviously belonging to a man, but I can't help wondering about the story behind all the everyday objects I come across. As I unpack a stack of espresso cups I wonder, did these belong to him? Did he like a fast coffee before he headed off to his high-powered advertising job? I find a guidebook listing London's best restaurants. Did Edie and my dad read through it together, highlighting the ones they wanted to try? And if so, did they ever get to try them or did he die before they got the chance? There are cushions. Several boxes containing nothing but scatter cushions. I wonder what my dad thought about them. I imagine him complaining about them, chucking them off the bed onto the floor.

When we're done, we flop down onto the sofa.

'I think that is a job well done, don't you?' Edie says. 'I reckon we need tea, we need cake and we need them now.' From nowhere, Edie produces a box of tea bags, a small bottle of milk and shop-bought carrot cake. 'I came prepared!'

Over our afternoon tea Edie chats happily away about her plans for the flat and the garden and how she's going to arrange the kitchen cupboard. When we're finished, I realise I should be heading home but I suddenly feel worried about Edie.

I can slip easily back into my other life – go home now, to school on Monday, business as usual – but what about Edie? Everything she's known for the last eight years has gone. Her boyfriend. Her house. She doesn't even have a job. What will she do when I go home? Watch telly? Make some dinner for one? I look over at where she's drying up mugs and placing them proudly in her new cupboard. She seems cheerful enough.

And then I tell myself to put my ego away. Edie doesn't need me. I'm just some kid she's only just met.

She is perfectly capable of looking after herself.

26

On Monday, I manage to annoy Mum through no real fault of my own when some important academic colleague rings on the house phone when she's out. The guy has an almost completely incomprehensible accent so although I do my best to take a detailed message to pass on to her, I manage to get both the name and the number wrong so Mum is in the dark about who it was or what he wanted.

'I mean, honestly, Anna, does Frankfurter sound like a plausible Christian name for a human male to you? Did you even try to listen properly?' she sighed as she keyed different combinations of numbers into the phone, trying desperately to find something that would work. 'If you'd at least got his name I could have looked him up. You've left me nothing to go on! Why can't you ever just *concentrate*?'

I left the kitchen then, making a big thing about slamming the door and stomping up the stairs, but Mum rarely notices these little protests.

I ignore her for the next two days, but she probably doesn't register that either.

Later in the week Edie texts me to ask if she can cook me

a special dinner to say thank you for all my help with the flat-hunting and the move. She also tells me she has a present for me. I can't think for the life of me what it could be but who am I to turn down a present and a free dinner? Especially as, since the phone message row, things at home have been about as comfortable as a nettle vest. We make a date for the following Wednesday.

When I arrive at the flat, I'm impressed with all the work that Edie's obviously put into getting the place together. She tells me she's been scouring charity shops, discount stores, 'everywhere – even skips sometimes!' and she's collected a mish-mash of odds and ends that, although maybe a bit eccentric, definitely make the place feel homely. She's made herself a bookshelf by resting a plank of wood on two small stacks of bricks and she's found a simple wooden dining table from somewhere and tucked it in the bay of the window to make a cute little dining area. All along the window sill she's lined up empty jam jars with candles inside and they fill the room with a gentle flickering light.

'Wow, Edie. It looks really nice in here.'

She stands back, looking around. 'Oh, do you think so? I'm so pleased. I've really done my best.'

'It looks great. Really great. Oh, I brought you something.' I reach into my pocket and pull out the little badge I bought off George earlier that day. It was probably the first time I had ever actually handed money over to him. 'It's the badge you wanted.'

Edie takes it from me and laughs. 'Trumpet nose! I love this! I love this one! What a clever thing. So funny!' She pins it to her apron then says, 'And I've got something for you, of course. Your present. Close your eyes, I'll get it.'

141

I do as I'm told and I hear Edie leave the room and return a few moments later. 'OK. Ready? Open!'

I'd been prepared to flash a delighted smile no matter what random knick-knack Edie presented me with, but when I open my eyes and see that Edie is holding out a real-life acoustic guitar, I don't need to pretend.

'Seriously? You bought that for me? A guitar?'

Edie nods enthusiastically. 'It was in a charity shop. Didn't have any strings, but easy enough to sort that. It's not the best model but not the worst either. Plenty good enough for a beginner. I've tuned her up, so you're ready to go!' She passes it to me and I rest it on my knee.

'Wow. Thank you, but . . . I mean, I can't play it.'

Edie does a mock affronted face. 'And what about that A minor I so carefully taught you?'

I peer down at the neck of the guitar and try to remember where to position my fingers. I look up to check with Edie. 'Like this?'

She laughs and shifts one of my fingers down a string. 'Almost. Now try.'

I strum and it actually sounds not too bad.

'Brilliant!' Edie says, grinning. 'Now try this.'

She lifts two of my fingers up one string each and removes one altogether. 'Right. Try that.'

I give it a go and this one sounds OK too.

'And that, my dear, is an almost-perfect E minor.'

I smile. 'Cool.' I practise swapping between the two chords and get a sort of clumsy rhythm going.

'I reckon that's basically a song you've got there,' Edie tells me, clapping along to the beat.

I laugh and swing the guitar off my knee. I lean it against the wall and stand back to look at it.

It's a nice looking thing, I think. Battered, but cool. I can't believe I've never thought about getting one before. I turn to Edie. 'Thank you so much, for getting me it. It's really great. Seriously.'

'It's my pleasure, my love.'

Edie heads into the kitchen to get our dinner ready. She's adamant I can't do anything to help so I fiddle around with my two new guitar chords and watch a bit of telly while she gets on with it. When it's ready, she lays it out on the little wooden dining table and I take my seat.

It turns out that Edie can really cook. She's really pushed the boat out. There are three beautiful courses – perfectly formed little onion tarts with this delicious chutney on the side, a kind of Asian-style chicken and noodle thing, and then a chocolate tart with raspberries all over the top.

'That was amazing,' I tell her when we're done, leaning back in my seat and wondering if it would be OK to undo the button on my jeans. 'You're definitely as good as a real, proper chef,' I tell her, and I'm not just saying it. 'Did you make it all yourself – like all the pastry and everything?'

Edie nods and looks a bit bashful. 'Well, I've got to be good at something, I suppose, and there's not much else I can do!' She does a small laugh but it fades quickly and then she gets a bit of a sad look in her eyes.

I hope I haven't upset her somehow. That wasn't what I intended. 'You can play the guitar,' I point out.

She smiles and nods, but she doesn't say anything. We're quiet for a moment and I don't know what to do next. I want

143

to reassure her, for her to stop looking so wistful and faraway, but I can't think of anything to say.

Suddenly she seems to snap out of it. 'You had a word with that boy yet, then?' She picks up a raspberry that's escaped her plate and rolled across the table. 'Told him to back off?'

I shake my head and look down at my plate.

'Is it . . . is it because in a way, you feel you deserve to be treated like this? Is it the guilt? Do you feel like this is your punishment so you just have to take it?'

This sounds a bit like trashy magazine psycho-babble to me but I give it some thought in case Edie has hit on something. I decide she hasn't, not really. I do feel bad about what happened to Shay and I wish more than anything I could go back and relive that day. I wish I could leave Shay wrestling the cat and not interfere, or that I had just never gone over to the Bradstock house at all. But I really didn't mean to hurt him. It's not like I lost my temper and now I'm regretting my actions. It was a genuine accident. I don't deserve to be punished for ever for that. Do I?

I shake my head. 'It's not really that. It's just that there's no point talking to Leon. What am I supposed to say? He won't take any notice of anything.'

Edie thinks for a moment. 'As I see it, he's basically all talk, right? I mean, he hasn't got anything to gain from dropping you in it, has he? How will he benefit from getting you in hot water with that little kid's father? He won't. He's just using it as a way – a pretty damn screwed-up way – of trying to win you over. I guess he's thinking that if he can force you to spend enough time with him that you'll . . . I don't know, fall for him, eventually.'

I let out an indignant snort. 'I will not.'

'No, I know,' Edie says. 'But I reckon that's his thinking. But if you just point-blank refuse to go anywhere with him, to even *speak* to him, why would he bother reporting you? That's not going to get him anywhere, is it? In fact, all it will mean is that he's ruled out any chance of ever being anywhere near friends with you.'

I think about this for a moment. The logic makes sense, I can see that, but instinct tells me it wouldn't quite work out like that. There's something Edie's not taking into account. I can't quite put my finger on it but it's something about how Leon's mind works. How he gets his kicks.

'I don't think he even likes me that much,' I try to explain. 'Not really. Not for who I really am. I think it's just like, I don't know . . . control. He likes to think he's important and that he can have whatever – or whoever – he wants. He's mental.'

Edie raises her eyebrows slightly but she doesn't say anything. I don't think I can really explain how someone like Leon operates. It wouldn't make sense to anyone. It definitely doesn't make sense to me.

I sigh. 'I don't know. Maybe it's worth a try.' It's true that I've never even tried to speak to Leon about the situation we're in. So far everything's been based on inferences and second-guessing and me hoping for the best. Maybe it is time I sat down with him and had it out properly.

Maybe it'd make him think about what he's actually trying to achieve.

27

The next time I see Leon is two days after my dinner with Edie. He's coming out of one of his writing club meetings and is making a big deal of saying goodbye to his Year Seven fans, shouting words of advice and encouragement – 'Take care, Tilly. Remember, one per cent inspiration, ninety-nine per cent perspiration!' Then he sees me. 'Ah! Anna!' he calls over the young ones' heads. 'What a lovely surprise. Long time no see.'

I don't think this is true. Not long enough, anyway.

He falls into step with me as I walk past. 'You know, I've been meaning to ask you for your thoughts on my piece in the magazine. I'd welcome your comments. All feedback is interesting, wherever it comes from!'

I keep walking quickly down the corridor. We turn from the busy main walkway into the quieter science area. The walls are panelled with dark wood here. It has a faint scent of Bunsen burners and sulphur.

'I haven't read it.' I don't make any effort to sound apologetic. If anything, I'm defiant. I'm kind of surprised by my own boldness.

'Ah. I see.' Leon's voice has an edge to it. He's close to tetchy but not quite there yet. He hasn't quite decided which way to go. He's giving me the benefit of the doubt. If I come up with a reasonable excuse for why I haven't looked at it yet, he'll let me off. But I'm not going to do that. I'm not going to lie this time.

'Leon.' I stop and turn to face him. It takes him by surprise. 'This has to stop. You can't make me want to be with you. It's no foundation for . . .' I don't know what to say. Friendship? A relationship? 'For anything. You know what happened was an accident. You can't keep this up for ever. It has to stop.'

Leon doesn't say anything for a moment. He just peers at me, like he's listening very hard, like I'm speaking in a strong accent or a strange dialect and he's having to concentrate to keep up. Then he suddenly lets out one short laugh: 'Ha!'

I hadn't expected that reaction.

Then he puts his arm around my shoulders and guides me to the edge of the corridor, where there's a little recess between two blocks of lockers.

'Oh, Anna,' he says, positioning himself opposite me and chuckling quietly. 'Oh, Anna.'

'What?' I still sound cross but I'm feeling nervous. I don't know what he's going to say next. Or what he's going to do. I feel trapped in this square of space he's manoeuvred me into.

He takes his phone out of his trouser pocket and presses a few buttons. I know what's coming. I don't want to see the clip again. I don't need to, I know what it shows.

I cover the phone with my hand and push it down, but he pushes back. He holds it up, making me watch. If anything, it's worse than I remember.

147

When it's finally finished, I look right at him. I don't let myself look away. I make myself stay there, facing him. 'This *has* to stop, Leon.' I want to sound firm and in control but my voice comes out pleading, pathetic.

Leon just laughs again. 'Oh, Anna.' He leans in close. I try to step backwards but I'm already up against the wall. His mouth is millimetres from my ear. He speaks in a low, creepy whisper. 'We're just getting started.'

Then, just as I think he's going to back off, he turns and kisses me on the cheek. I jerk my head back, hitting it on the wall behind me. Leon just smiles and turns and then he's gone. I stand there, my eyes stinging with hot tears. I'm furious. I hate him so much.

I stay there in the gap between the lockers for a few minutes, making myself breathe slowly, blinking until the tears are gone. Then I step out of the recess and walk quickly down the corridor, out of the science department and out of school. I don't tell anyone that I'm leaving. I don't go back to collect my coat. I just keep walking and walking until I get to Denmark Run.

Edie is at home, which is lucky. She's surprised to see me, shivering, damp and coatless on her doorstep in the middle of the day, but she lets me in and makes me hot chocolate and waits for me to tell her what I'm doing there. I tell her the whole thing – exactly what I said to Leon and what he said to me. I tell her about the video on his phone and about that sickening, intrusive kiss.

When I've got the whole thing out it hits me for the first time what people mean when they talk about a problem shared being a problem halved. I've always thought it was a stupid concept before – surely a problem shared is a problem doubled if it means that now two people have to deal with it? – but sitting here now with Edie, I feel a real, physical relief. I feel lighter.

Edie doesn't do much at first. She just says, 'I see,' and takes a sip of her tea. Then she sits and thinks, her face grim.

It occurs to me then how different Edie is from all the other people in my life. If I'd told one of them – George or Sienna or Mum – they would've reacted straight away. George and Sienna would've laid into Leon, ranted about what a creep he was. They would've told me off too – called me 'soft' for encouraging him. Mum would've blamed me too, I expect. Or accused me of exaggerating the situation. I realise how glad I am that I chose to come to Edie. I realise how grateful I am that I had the option. If this had happened a few months ago, I wouldn't have even known her.

'I think the best thing,' Edie says eventually, 'is to steer clear. For the time being, at least. Emotions are running high. You don't want to aggravate the situation. Just lie low, avoid any confrontation. Give yourself a breather.'

This is exactly the advice I want to hear. All I want to do right now is hide. I don't want to face anyone. I just want to curl up and pretend Leon doesn't exist. I want to pretend that *I* don't exist.

Edie lets me stay at her flat for the rest of the day and into the evening. We don't talk about Leon or Shay or anything very much. We play a bit of guitar – she teaches me two new chords – and she makes me a tuna sandwich and lots of cups of tea. She disappears into her bedroom for a while and potters around sorting out drawers and shelves. I curl up in the corner of her sofa and work my way through her *Friends* box set. I don't let myself think about anything except the telly. I force my brain to stay empty of all thoughts and feelings.

Eventually, when it's been dark for several hours, I head home. I know Mum will be safely in her study by now. I slip upstairs without making a sound and get straight into bed.

28

Over the next few weeks Edie's flat – and Edie herself – become a kind of refuge to me. She gets a job –'Thanks to that wonderful CV you did for me!' – in a shop that sells handmade fudge. I often drop in there on my way home from school. When it isn't too busy, I sit behind the counter in the sweet buttery fog and Edie tells me lively stories about her customers and slips me bits of fudge until I feel sick. The boy who drives the delivery van, Isaac, is only a few years older than me and sometimes he comes in too and makes us both laugh by telling us about his crazy house full of sisters and cousins and nephews. At the end of Edie's shift we amble back to her flat together and she makes us a tray of tea and biscuits, and then later, usually dinner too.

At home, it seems like Mum and I can now go for days, even weeks, without really speaking to each other at all. It feels like we're more distant than ever. I suppose this is partly because I'm out so much of the time but it's also because she's spending more time than ever in her study. From the snatches of phone conversations I overhear, I gather that the planning for her conference is still going on but that it's not going as well as it should be. I know better than to ask about it though. I know from experience that when Mum is not happy, she'll take it out on anyone who happens to be there so the best thing I can do is *not* be there. We live our lives separately, moving around each other like trains in a model railway, gliding on our own rails of routine from our bedrooms to the kitchen to the bathroom and back again, but never really meeting. Even if I did want to tell her about Dad's death or about Edie, I'm not sure it would be that easy to find an opportunity.

I manage to avoid Leon for a few weeks after the video-and-kiss episode in the science corridor, but then he obviously realises he hasn't seen me for a while and starts to seek me out again. Just like last time, after our row outside the Henry McCain talk, he acts like our little confrontation never happened at all.

In the weeks leading up to Christmas he turns his attention to editing and perfecting the novel he tried and failed to show to Henry McCain, believing that with some fine-tuning he could have something 'really quite special' on his hands. He starts printing out pages that he's particularly proud of and bringing them to me for my 'critique'. I'm no expert but it all looks like rubbish to me. Sentences seem to drag on for whole pages without so much as a comma, and half the time I feel like he's just copied out lists of adjectives from a thesaurus. Nevertheless, I'm always careful to be complimentary and encouraging. It's just so much easier to say whatever he wants to hear. I've given up any ideas about standing up to him. I just can't face it and, in any case, I know there's no point.

It often seems funny to me, that Leon should be so pleased by my positive comments on his writing, when he knows full well I have to keep him onside. How can compliments made under duress mean anything to him?

One evening in early January, just after I've gone back to school for the new term, Edie calls to ask if I want to come over to her place for dinner and films on Saturday night. It sounds like a pleasant enough way to spend an evening so I'm about to accept when I remember what date it is on Saturday. 'It's my birthday that day actually. I'm sixteen.'

'Oh! All the more reason, then!' Edie says. 'I can make you something special!'

I am tempted. I've never really been big on birthdays – being the centre of attention makes me uncomfortable and I always feel under pressure to look more cheerful and excited than I'm feeling. Having a quiet evening with Edie's amazing food sounds like a pretty ideal way to get it out the way, but I'm also all too aware of what George and Sienna would make of that plan.

I've barely mentioned Edie at all after I laid into Sienna about her that time in Sienna's room. I'm pretty sure they both know I still see her occasionally but I don't think they know quite how much time I'm spending at her place. Things have been a bit weird between the three of us for a while now. I know it's my fault. Not because of the row between Sienna and me – I texted her a lame apology the day after and luckily Sienna finds arguments 'horribly tedious' so she didn't hold a grudge – but because I know I'm keeping them at arm's length, not joining in like I used to.

It was bad enough when I was just keeping the whole Leon blackmail issue a secret from them, but now I'm trying not to mention when I'm seeing Edie either, I feel like I'm constantly having to watch what I say around them. With them not knowing about some of the biggest things going on in my life, I guess I just don't feel that close to them at the moment and, if I'm honest, that makes me sad. I know if I tell them that I'm choosing to spend my sixteenth birthday with Edie rather than them, it could spell the beginning of the end of things between us.

'I can't,' I tell Edie. 'I'm really sorry. It does sound nice but I've got plans with my friends. I haven't seen that much of them lately so . . .'

'Oh, of course, of course.' If Edie's disappointed she doesn't let it show. 'You want to be with your friends on your sixteenth! Of course you do.'

Although I haven't actually made any official plans with George and Sienna yet, I assume they will already have my birthday on their radar and will probably have a few ideas about what we should do. I'd be perfectly happy with some snacks and films round one of their houses, just sitting around and taking the piss out of each other. Just being normal together, like we used to. But when I bring this idea up with them on the bus home the following day, I'm surprised and annoyed to see they don't look at all keen.

George looks at Sienna but she just shrugs.

'What?' I demand. 'What is it?'

'It's just that we're kind of *busy* on Saturday night, Spanner . . .' George says.

He looks to Sienna for support and she steps in. 'We're going to this gig thing in town. It was kind of last minute. Archie got us tickets.' Then she adds quickly, 'I mean, we didn't forget your birthday or anything. God, no! It's just we just thought you'd be busy . . . You just seem to . . . have a lot on at the moment.'

'It's fine,' I say, turning away from them and looking out the window. 'Don't worry about it. It was just an idea.'

They're quiet for a minute and I can tell they're mouthing at each other behind my back.

George gets up and comes and takes the seat next to me. He rests his head on my shoulder and looks up at me with puppy-dog eyes. 'Don't be mad, Spanner.'

'I'm not.' I dip my shoulder to wriggle him off. 'It's fine.'

'What about the Friday?' he says. 'Let's do the Friday. Come to Sienna's. I'll bring the films. We'll get her dad to fire up the outside pizza oven. We'll have cake. It'll be awesome.'

I force a smile. 'OK. Sure. Sounds good.'

29

As I walk from the bus stop to my house, I figure that now I've tried to be a normal teenager and see my friends on my birthday and my friends have turned me down, I might as well go ahead and accept Edie's invitation to have dinner with her on Saturday. Assuming, that is, that it still stands. I feel pretty confident that it will. I decide to text her later.

When I get home, I'm surprised to find Mum in the kitchen and even more surprised to find that she seems to be in a good mood.

'Good day?' I ask.

She nods. 'Yes. Absolutely a good day.' Mum launches into a very long and convoluted story about the conference and a professor from Poland and a paper and a research grant. I don't really follow it entirely but I try to show interest and look pleased. It's the most we've spoken in weeks.

When she's finished her story, she goes over and starts to empty the dishwasher. 'So,' she says. 'Sixteen years. Sixteen!'

It takes me a minute but I realise she's talking about my birthday. 'Oh, yeah. Saturday.'

She shakes her head like she can't believe it. 'Sixteen years old. My word.' She goes over to the sink, makes me a glass of squash that I didn't ask for, and puts it down on the table in front of me. 'I tell you what – I'll cook for you. Whatever you want. How about that?' She goes over to the dresser where she keeps her handbag and takes out her purse. She pulls out a twenty-pound note and pushes it into my hand. 'Here. You go to the shops and choose whatever you want to eat – chicken, fish, steak, lobster, caviar . . . whatever you want. I'll cook it for you. We'll have a special birthday meal, just the two of us, eh?'

I'm almost lost for words. It's been a very long time since Mum has shown this much interest in me. For the last four years or so, when my birthday's come around, she's just whipped out a tenner the day before and told me to get whatever I want as a present. On my fifteenth birthday she didn't even remember to say happy birthday to me on the day at all. It was only two days later, when she was flicking through her diary, that she looked up and said, 'Oh, it was Friday! Happy birthday for then. Did you have a good day?'

I know this sudden show of interest is only because she's in a good mood. It's just because her work is going well, rather than because she's decided she actually is pleased to have a daughter after all, but frankly I'll take what I can get. And now she's making the effort, it seems only right to be gracious about it.

'OK. Great. That sounds nice.'

The Friday before my birthday, I go to Sienna's for pizzas and films as planned. Her parents make a fuss of me, her dad making a big show of inventing a pizza topping just for me – the 'Spanneroni' – and Sienna and George have made me a cake, this time minus the offensive slogan.

We lounge around in Sienna's room and watch dodgy comedies and eat junk and from the outside at least, it seems very much like old times. I guess they're feeling guilty about ditching me on my birthday and I'm feeling guilty about neglecting them so we're all trying extra hard to be nice to each other, to convince ourselves that things are normal. Maybe things are normal; I don't know. What is normal now? Is it normal to stay the same for ever?

On Saturday morning, I wake up late and listen to the rain pummelling my window. Well then, I think. Look at me. Sixteen years old. I swing my legs out from under my duvet and sit on the edge of my bed looking at myself in the mirror. I try to think of what I can do now that I couldn't do yesterday. I can only come up with having sex or joining the army. Neither immediately appeal.

I go down to the kitchen, pour myself a bowl of Frosties and think about what to do with myself. I feel like I should do something with the day, but I haven't got plans with Mum until later. I'm pretty sure that if she's taking the whole evening off to cook and eat with me that she'll be hard at it in her study all day to make up for it, so really I should stay out of her way.

I think about going to see George and Sienna but they haven't asked me what I'm doing in the day, and it feels wrong that a person should have to ask for company on their own sixteenth birthday, so instead I watch junk on telly and read the internet while I wait for the rain to stop.

When it seems to have cleared up outside, I decide it's time to head down to the shops to choose the things I want for my special birthday dinner with Mum. As I've got plenty of time to kill, rather than heading straight to the supermarket, I decide to go into town and do a tour of the little delis, greengrocers and fishmongers on the high street. It'll be proper shopping, I think, like people did in the olden days.

Once I get going, I find I'm quite enjoying the task. I go to Coco's, a French delicatessen hidden away down a side road and spend ages looking at the interesting jars and packages. I eventually come out with some potent French cheeses and a jar of plum chutney. After the deli I head to the greengrocers for a random selection of vegetables – squash, kale, beetroot. Kohlrabi, whatever that is. I'm not sure exactly what meal I'm planning for, but I imagine it'll all come together in the end. I pick up some enormous king prawns from the fishmongers then call in at George's parents' shop. I hope that Sally and Pete might say happy birthday to me or even slip me a freebie, but when I get there I find they're not working today. Instead there's a new girl on, some miserable-looking emo type. She packs up my box of cupcakes without saying a word.

I've gone well over my twenty pound budget, but I don't really care. I've enjoyed my little expedition and I'm actually really looking forward to my dinner. As I struggle down the road to the house, the heavy carrier bags cutting into my fingers, I feel a sudden surge of hope. Maybe, I think, tonight will be a turning point for me and Mum. It's always seemed to me that Mum wasn't really the type of person to get on with children – she's too serious, too clever. Too impatient. But now I'm getting older, basically an adult for all intents and purposes, maybe this will be where we start to forge a relationship. Maybe if I show Mum how different I am now, that I'm not just some irritating little kid to keep her from her work, that I'm intelligent and mature, that I appreciate the importance of what she does, maybe she'll start to see me in a new light. Maybe we'll never have a traditional mother/daughter relationship, but maybe she'll have more respect for me. She'll think of me as an equal. Maybe it's even time I told her about Dad. I'd leave it till the end of the night, of course – don't want to put a downer on the evening – but tonight could be the perfect time.

By the time I get home, it's nearly dark outside and I expect that Mum will be out of her study by now, maybe pottering around the kitchen, getting things ready for the evening. But when I push the front door open, struggling to turn the key with the heavy bags in my hands, I find the house dark and silent. I dump the bags on the table in the kitchen and head upstairs to her study, figuring she's probably just lost track of time. But when I get to the door, I find it open. The lights are off and her desk is clear. She must've gone into work, I realise. She sometimes heads to the lab on a Saturday when she can work without students getting under her feet. Still, she'll be home soon.

I head back downstairs and put a few lamps on. I choose a CD of upbeat music – some Caribbean band I've never heard of – and slip it into Mum's stereo, trying to get a bit of a party mood going. I look over at the bags of food on the table and wonder if I should start doing some food preparation. No, I think, best leave it. I'm no cook and I don't want to mess up the good ingredients before Mum's even got started. I make myself a drink, take a magazine from the basket by the door and sit down at the table to wait.

I wait for two and a half hours.

It's seven o'clock and I have no idea where Mum is. I try to fight the creeping feeling of irritation because I don't want to put myself in a bad mood for the evening, but it's hard – did she really have to go into work today? Couldn't she just *not* work, just for one day? Normally I know better than to bother her when she's busy, but I figure this is a special case. I call her mobile.

'Yes?' She sounds impatient. There's a lot of background noise.

'Mum? Where are you?'

'Anna? I'm in Krakow. Didn't you get my note?'

It takes me a minute to process this. 'What note? What do you mean, Krakow? As in Poland?'

'Exactly.'

'What are you doing there?'

'Professor Baranski requested a meeting. We've got a few last-minute things to clear up. I'm sorry about dinner. All a bit of a rush. We'll do it next weekend, or some other time, I'm sure.'

It slowly sinks in that she's not going to be home this evening.

'I explained it all in the note anyway,' she says, sounding a bit impatient now. 'On the kitchen table.'

I carry the phone with me over to the kitchen table. I lift up the bag of cheese and vegetables I dropped there earlier, and see the message, scrawled on the back of an unopened electricity bill.

Anna,

So sorry, something's come up. Got to fly to Poland tonight. Bit of a mad rush, but could be exciting news!! Happy birthday, have a good night – ask your friends to come over.
Mum

On the other end of the phone, I hear a man's voice and then Mum say, 'Yes, coming now. Sorry.'

I hang up on her. She clearly hasn't even got time for a phone call with me, much less dinner.

I just sit there for a minute, looking stupidly at the phone in my hand. I imagine if this were a film or if I were a more emotional person, I might hurl it across the room at this point, but it's not and I'm not so I just drop it back into its cradle. I pick up the bags of cheese and chutney and beetroot and cake and I shove the whole lot haphazardly in the fridge. I don't want to look at them. I don't want to remember how carefully I picked everything out, honestly believing that Mum was going to make this evening special for me. I feel like a total idiot.

I pick the phone back up and dial George's number.

'Hello?'

'Hey!' I try to sound especially cheerful. I try to sound like someone you'd want to hang out with. 'How's it going? What time are you guys going to the gig?'

'We're on our way!' In the background I can hear Sienna asking who it is.

'Can I come?'

There's an awkward pause. 'Uh . . . tickets are sold out, dude.'

'Ah, right. OK. No worries.'

'I thought your mum was cooking you your special meal and all that?'

'Oh yeah, she is. I was just thinking like, after, maybe we could . . . but no, it's cool. Don't worry. Have a good night!'

I sit down on the kitchen chair. The cheerful steel band music is still tinkling away. I stand up and shut it off.

Then I turn out the lamps, collect my bags of food from the fridge and I leave the house.

30

As I stand on Edie's doorstep trying to stop a rogue block of cheese from breaking free of its bag, I worry that she might not be home. I'd just assumed she would be because she never really mentions any friends or activities she does in the evening, but is that because I don't ask? I decide there and then that I must make an effort to show more interest in Edie, to ask her more questions and check she's OK. After all, at the moment she's the only person who seems at all interested in me. Unless you count Leon, which I'd really rather not.

She is home. When she opens the door, she looks understandably surprised to see me. I say hello and sorry, but then it's my turn to be surprised because I notice what she's wearing: she seems to be dressed in some kind of historical costume. It's true that her clothes are always a little on the quirky side but this evening she's really taken things up a level – she's wearing a long, white, smock-style dress with frills around the cuffs, pale green gloves up to her elbows and a pink bonnet. It's all very Little Bo Peep.

'Anna?' She pulls the door open wide. 'What's wrong, is everything OK?'

I'm awkward for a moment. Maybe I shouldn't have come. What *is* she wearing?

'I thought you were with your mum tonight? Oh! And happy birthday, of course!' She reaches forward to give me a hug but with the heavy bags in my hands, it nearly knocks me over. 'Whoops a daisy!' She laughs, taking the bags from me. She peers inside them. 'Blimey O'Reilly, what have you got here? Enough food to sink a ship!'

I follow Edie into the kitchen. 'Mum had to work, but I'd already bought the food, so . . .' I shrug. I feel silly. I shouldn't have just turned up like this. What an idiot.

Edie looks from my face to the bags and back again. I see something clock in her eyes. 'Ah. I see. Well, never mind! Sometimes these things happen, eh? But not to worry. You've got a right lot of lovely stuff here. I'm sure I can rustle you up something delicious in no time. Why don't you sort us out some drinks and I'll get to work. We'll have a proper little party!'

I smile shyly and take two glasses out of the cupboard. 'Thanks, Edie.'

She gives my arm a squeeze. 'Silly.'

I pour us a glass of Coke each and put Edie's down on the side next to her chopping board. 'I like your dress . . .' I say carefully. I'm *pretty* sure it's some kind of fancy dress this time but you can never quite tell with Edie.

'Oh!' she says, looking down like she'd forgotten she had it on. 'It's my Regency look. I was going to have a *Pride and Prejudice* night – the whole box set – and it's always more fun if I look the part!'

I can't help but smile, and she looks embarrassed suddenly. 'Oh, blimey, I'm mad, aren't I? You think I'm mad. I'll go and take it off . . .'

'No.' I put my hand on her arm. 'No, don't. I love it. It's a great idea. It's fun. In fact . . . don't suppose you've got another?'

Edie's eyes light up. 'I've not got another frock, no, but I tell you what I have got . . .' She's already disappeared into her room. After a bit of shuffling around and opening and closing of drawers, she comes back. She's holding another costume. There's a dark jacket with tails, some little white trousers and ruffly neck thing. At first I think it's some sort of admiral costume, but then I realise. 'Mr Darcy?'

Edie smiles. 'Exactly! What do you reckon?'

I nod slowly and take the hanger from her. 'I think I could pull it off.'

'Oh, for sure,' Edie says. 'I think you'll look quite dashing.'

I go into the bathroom to put it on and leave Edie chopping in the kitchen. Once I've got the costume on I look in the mirror. I look so ridiculous and the whole evening – me in here, wearing this; Edie out there, in that bonnet – all seems so totally crackers that I get a massive attack of the giggles. I go out to the kitchen and when Edie sees me she starts laughing too, and we carry on like that for about ten minutes. We'll just stop laughing and get our breath back and then one of us will catch the other's eye and we'll start all over again. I honestly can't remember the last time I laughed so much or so hard.

Edie tells me that the ingredients I've bought are a 'little bit disjointed' so she cooks us a 'tasting menu' – lots of little delicious dishes on tiny plates. We eat on our laps watching *Pride and Prejudice* right from the beginning. Every so often Edie will pause the DVD and make me repeat one of Mr Darcy's lines in my best posh accent. If I don't try hard enough or make it dramatic enough she makes me stand up and do it again and soon my impressions are so over-the-top and silly I can't get to the end of a sentence without dissolving into giggles.

When Edie has cleared away our plates from course number three and has headed back to the kitchen area, I have a sudden thought. I don't know where it comes from, but it hits me so hard that I say it aloud before I've had a chance to think about what I'm doing.

'Did this costume belong to my dad?'

Edie freezes, one hand on a cupboard handle. Her mouth is hanging slightly open. I feel surprised too – almost as if someone else had asked that question. I can physically feel the change of atmosphere in the room. The DVD is paused so we stand there in silence for a second or two.

'No!' Edie says eventually. 'No! I wouldn't make you . . . Give you . . . No. No.' She turns back to the sink and busies herself washing some spoons. When she turns back to face me again she seems calmed. 'It's not his. Honestly.' Then she looks bashful. 'They just came as part of a set, the pair of them. Sometimes I'm Elizabeth, sometimes Mr Darcy . . .'

I laugh then, mostly out of nervousness I think, and so does Edie. The tension in the room eases slightly, but it still feels different now. I've gone and made things awkward, bringing up the dead dad like that.

We're both quiet for a moment while Edie fiddles around in the kitchen and I pretend to flick through a TV guide. Then

Edie says, 'Are you cross with your mum for going away today? Has she upset you?'

My first instinct is to say no, to brush the question away and explain that it's not a big deal, but then for some reason, I just don't want to. I *am* angry and I *am* upset and I'm not going to pretend otherwise.

I drop the TV guide to the floor and turn to face Edie. 'It was her idea, the whole thing. That's what really pisses me off. I could've found something else to do tonight but she was all like, "Go and get all your favourites, it'll be a special dinner, just you and me, blah blah blah". Why does she even *say* stuff like that if she has no intention of actually doing it? I wouldn't have expected anything, otherwise. I know she doesn't even like me.'

Edie doesn't say anything for a while. She just looks at me, like she's letting me get it all out. When I stop talking, she's frowning slightly. I can see her thinking about how to reply. I realise this is a weird position for her to be in. I mean, surely Edie must hate my mum, just as a matter of course? I'm pretty sure my dad will have told her that my mum was a total bitch to him and she'll probably have believed him. It's only natural for someone to hate their partner's ex, right? So now here I am, laying into Mum, telling Edie what a cow she's been, Edie must want to join in, mustn't she? It must be tempting for her to agree.

Edie comes back over to the sofa and sits down with me. 'It must be hard, I think,' she says carefully. 'To be a single parent. I know I can't even look after myself half the time!' She laughs but I don't join in so she stops.

I suddenly wish we weren't wearing these stupid costumes. I pull at my frilly neckerchief, trying to loosen it.

'I suppose, what you have to remember,' Edie goes on, 'what you have to bear in mind, is that when you were born, I suppose, your mum wasn't in the best place, emotionally speaking. I know it had been a tough few months.'

'You mean, with my grandma being ill?'

I know my grandmother – Mum's mum – died just before I was born. I suppose I'm kind of surprised that Edie knows this though. Obviously my father liked to talk about the past more than my mother does.

'Yes, and then there was the timing and everything she'd given up to have you. She'd planned the timing of the pregnancy so carefully and so I suppose when it didn't work out . . .'

'What plans? I was a mistake, I'm sure of it. There's no way that Mum would've *planned* to get pregnant right in the middle of her course.'

Mum found out she was pregnant when she was halfway through her Masters degree. She'd had to drop out, reapply and complete the entire thing again. The whole episode must've set her career back by nearly three years in total and I've always had a pretty good idea that Mum resents me for that. I've always assumed it's part of the reason she seems to find me so irritating.

Edie frowns and shakes her head. 'Definitely not a mistake. Very planned. Very, very planned.'

'What do you mean, "very planned"?'

This seems like a strange phrasing. I wonder what she's getting at.

Edie peers at me, her eyes slightly narrowed. 'You mean, you don't know . . .? How much do you know, about that time? You do know what happened, don't you?'

31

I shrug. 'I don't know. What's there to know? Mum got pregnant by mistake. It messed up her education. She had me. She's blamed me ever since.'

Edie shakes her head. 'Oh, no. No! That's not it at all. I can't believe you don't know . . . Well, anyway. It's ever such a sweet story, but sad too.'

Edie tells me that Mum was twenty-one when she found out that her mother was sick with the lung cancer that would eventually kill her – 'and you know how your mum adored her mother.'

I think about this. I know Mum speaks highly of her own mother, but to me, that's always seemed more like intellectual respect than anything more emotional. She has a photo of her – Professor Beatrix Castella – in her study, but it's not a smiling family photo of her with her husband and her children, or anything like that. It's a professional shot, taken during one of her lectures. She's standing at the front of an enormous lecture hall, looking important and formidable. Whenever Mum talks about her mother – which isn't really that often – she'll say things like 'she was one of the smartest thinkers of her generation' or she'll tell me a list of the awards she won but, really, she could be talking about any old academic, someone she'd never met, even. She's certainly never mentioned that she 'adored' her. I don't say this now though; I just nod so that Edie will go on speaking.

Edie explains that when my grandmother realised she wasn't going to recover from her cancer, she told mum she was full of regrets, and that she'd give up all her professional accolades if she could go back and have more time with her family. She told Mum that her greatest regret of all was that she would never get to meet her grandchildren.

'And the way James always described it,' Edie goes on, 'is that your mum sort of got it into her head that if she got pregnant right there and then, or as soon as possible anyway, that she could give her mother a reason to hang on. Like she imagined her mum might kind of *will* herself not to die, so she could see her grandchild. And so, even though James wasn't sure about the plan, and even though it meant Anita had to give up her place on her course, put her career on hold, all the rest of it, they set out to have a baby, just as soon as they possibly could. They set out to have you. Do you see?' Edie looks at me earnestly. 'You *were* planned. Very planned.'

Edie's smiling like she's just delivered some brilliant news, like she expects me to smile back, to be relieved and delighted to find out I was wanted after all. But what she doesn't seem to realise is that she's missing the whole point.

I look back at her. I'm not smiling. 'But it didn't work, did it? My grandmother died before I was born. Maybe I was part of a plan, but it was a failed plan.'

Edie blinks in surprise, like this interpretation hadn't occurred to her. Then she looks sad, disappointed that her story hasn't had the effect she was hoping for. 'Well, I suppose . . .'

'Really,' I say, in a bitter voice, 'I was already an enormous disappointment to everyone, before I was even born.'

I sound angry, but I just feel sad. I feel sad that my grandmother never got to meet me. I feel sad that she died so young when she was still doing great things, but that those great things weren't enough to stop her having regrets. I feel sad that Mum's plan didn't work out, when she'd given up so much for it. I feel sad that Mum and her mum obviously liked each other a whole lot more than she's ever liked me.

It just doesn't seem fair that so much should be messed up before I even got a chance to get involved.

32

Edie seems uncomfortable. I guess she's wishing she'd never brought the whole thing up. 'Well, I mean it's tragic, obviously, but my point is, you *were* planned . . .'

I don't reply. I don't want to talk about it any more.

The rest of the evening passes peacefully enough and we round things off with some of the stinking cheese I got from the deli. By the time we've finished eating it's late and I don't fancy the thought of walking home on my own only to arrive at an empty house so Edie makes me up a bed on the sofa. 'If I'd known you were going to stay, I'd have cleared out the back room,' she tells me as she shoves pillows into pillowcases, 'but it's so full of junk you wouldn't even be able to lie down.'

The next morning, Edie insists on making me breakfast before I go home. She says I can have anything I want and I ask for eggs, because it's the first thing I think of.

'No problem. I can do eggs. Boiled, fried, poached? I've got the whole repertoire.'

'No one can make poached eggs,' I point out. 'Everyone tries but it never works out. Never. You always just end up with snot in a pan of water.'

Edie laughs. 'I'll have you know I make perfect poached eggs!'

And she does. Not that I'm really surprised.

After breakfast, I reluctantly drag myself out into the frosty January morning and make my way home. When I get back to the house, it's cold and silent, just as I knew it would be, so I take my laptop to bed with me and pass most of the day looking up cartoons from my childhood and seeing which of the theme tunes I can still sing along to.

That evening, Mum comes home. She comes to my room to say hello, which is unusual – and more unusual still, she seems cheerful.

'So how was your trip?' I ask. There's just no point starting a row about the missed birthday dinner. It won't achieve anything.

'Good. Good! I saw Eryk Baranski obviously, but then Professor Chovanec turned up as well, which is quite the event because he rarely makes a personal appearance. I'd say we made some real strides forward, definitely.'

I imagine Mum and these two professor types taking literal giant strides around some big university building, their legs stretched out wide, and the thought makes me want to giggle. I don't though; I just say, 'Cool. Sounds good,' because that seems like the safest thing to do.

I expect Mum to disappear up to her study but instead she steps further into my room. She holds out a paper bag. 'I got you something. For your birthday. To make up for missing dinner. I am sorry about that, you know.' I take the paper bag and reach inside. It's a book. I slip it out. *Acoustic Polish Folk Tunes.*

'I've heard you practising,' she says. She seems shy suddenly, awkward. It's most unlike her.

I'm surprised she's even noticed me fiddling away with the battered old guitar in my room. And touched, in a way. 'Thank you. It's great.'

Mum does head to her study then and I stay in bed, just looking at the ceiling and feeling sad. I feel sad about everything – about Mum's plan that never worked out, about my dead grandma. Even about my dead dad. Then I don't know if it's nostalgia that makes me do it or more a longing for something that never happened in the first place, but I pull open my bottom drawer and take out the small pile of photos I keep in there, and spread them out across my pillow.

They're mostly of me and Mum when I was little. Mum always looks awkward – I know it's because she hates having her photo taken but it looks as if she's uncomfortable being so close to me, having my chubby toddler arms around her neck. Then I reach for my wallet and search through to the pocket in the back where – for reasons I don't quite understand myself – I keep the one picture I have of all three of us. The one photo of me, Mum and Dad together, sitting on a wall in front of a beach I don't know the name of, on a holiday I can't remember having.

But I can't find the photo.

I remember thinking at one point that I should probably take it out and keep it in the drawer so it doesn't get wet or lost, but I can't find it in the pile of photos from the drawer either. I half-heartedly shuffle through a few of my other drawers but I don't expect to find it. It's gone, I realise – and really, what does it matter? The family it shows – happy, relaxed, together – doesn't exist anyway. It never existed. I might as

175

well carry around a photo of Homer and Marge Simpson and pretend they're my parents.

I put my wallet away and get back into bed. I turn out the light and listen to the rain on the window. It's only as I'm drifting off to sleep that I remember Leon, standing in my room with that book, then him flashing me his wallet, showing me – showing off – that he'd stolen that photo of me. The thought of it wakes me up with a jolt. I imagine him rifling through the drawer next to my bed, helping himself to whatever he wants, that smug look on his face. A photo of me is one thing, but what kind of sick creep would steal the one photo I have of my dad? I hate him, I hate him, I hate him.

I sit up and take my phone from the bedside table. I send a message to Edie:

I can't cope with Leon any more.

I expect Edie to ring or to text back with questions – Why? What's happened? What's brought this on? – but she just replies with one sentence:

We'll think of something.

It's two days later and I'm walking to school when I get another text from her:

*I've found something. Could be the end to your Leon troubles!
Come over when you can and I'll explain.*

I'm intrigued but the truth is, I don't know if I feel convinced that Edie really has found the solution to all my problems. The thing with Edie is that she can be kind of naive. She's enthusiastic and excitable, which is great fun, but sometimes I don't know that she thinks things through entirely. Still, there might be something we can work with, I suppose. At the very least, an evening at Edie's means a night of guaranteed good food and a temporary escape from having to think about anything else, so I head home to dump my school stuff and get changed, ready to head over.

In my bedroom, as I take my phone and wallet out of my schoolbag and put them on my desk I notice that I have three missed calls, all within the last hour and all from a number I don't recognise. I check my voicemail but they haven't left a message. I figure it must be a junk call but as I go to shove the phone back into my pocket, it starts to ring again. It's the same number. I'm curious.

'Hello?'

'Anna? Is that Anna?' It's a man. I don't recognise his voice.

'Uh, yeah. Speaking.' I always feel stupid saying that.

'God, Anna.'

Who is this weirdo? I think about hanging up, but I know it'll bug me for hours if I don't find out who it is. 'Who is this, please?'

'Anna, it's James here. James Roddick. It's your father.'

33

I don't say anything. I sit down on my bed. I feel dizzy.

'Anna? Are you there?'

I take the phone away from my ear and look at the number on the screen again. It's an area code I don't recognise.

'Anna?'

I end the call.

Within a few seconds, the phone rings again. I cancel the call immediately. A few moments after that, I get a notification: he's left a voicemail. I think about deleting it, but then I'll never know. I'll never know who it was or what he wanted. I know I need to listen to it.

'Anna. I'm sorry, I know this must come as a surprise if she's told you what I think she's told you – and knowing her she probably has and . . .' He pauses, breathing out like he's trying to calm himself. 'Anna. Listen to me. You cannot trust Edie Southwood. She's a lunatic. Stay away from her. Please, call me. Please. I'll explain.'

I just sit there, looking at my phone's blank screen. My skin feels prickly and my heart is beating fast. I listen to the voicemail again, to check I really heard what I think I heard.

I try to make myself think rationally about this. Either that was not my father at all – that was another man, lying, trying to pull off some kind of con, maybe. Or, that *was* my father, and Edie – or whoever she really is – has told me one of the weirdest, most messed-up lies in history. I don't want to call him back. I don't want to speak to him while I'm in the dark. I don't want to be completely in his hands. Instead, I go over to my laptop and do something I can't believe I haven't done before. I search for my dad's name.

It turns out that there are hundreds of James Roddicks out there – none of them anything to do with me or my dad. American teenagers, an Australian cricket player. There's a story about a murder, which catches my eye and makes my skin prickle – until I click the link and find out that the James Roddick in the article was thrown under a train by a gang of robbers in 1895. I try to think how I can narrow it down, what else I can add to the search. Edie said he worked in advertising. I try James Roddick Advertising.

The first few links are useless again, but about a third of a way down the page the image search results show photos of men and boys – black, white, young, old. All these other James Roddicks. But the fourth one in the row makes my stomach do a kind of backflip. I recognise it straight away. It's the older, greyer and thinner version of my dad that I saw in Edie's photo, but it's definitely him. Definitely.

I click the image and it takes me to the Staff page of a website for some marketing company who specialise in 'targeted digital solutions', whatever that means. There isn't any more information on my dad, just the photo, his name and his job title: 'Business Development Executive'.

I wonder what people normally do with these kinds of pages. Wouldn't they have taken down my dad's photo by now if he was dead? Or would that seem harsh? Would they leave it up for a few months, then quietly remove it and hope no one noticed that one day it had been there and another day it was gone? But it's been months, months and months. Surely they would've updated the page by now? Unless it's one of those websites that no one really looks after and it's been left there out of laziness rather than respect . . .

I sit there for ages, thinking through all the possibilities, reading all the names of the other people who work at the company and wondering if they knew my dad, what they thought about him, whether they were friends – but then I start to annoy myself. There's an easy way to find out the truth here. I dial the number shown on the website's banner. My heart is beating hard.

'Good afternoon, Limelight Media?'

'Uh, hi, I was wondering, does James Roddick work there?'

I realise straight away that this is a weird question to ask – any genuine business associate would surely know the answer. The receptionist doesn't seem bothered though. 'James? Sure, do you want me to put you through?'

I'm about to say no – I'm definitely not ready to speak to him – but the receptionist jumps in, corrects herself.

'Oh, actually, you know what, he's out with clients this afternoon. Do you want me to get him to call you back?'

'No . . . no, thank you. It's fine. But, just to confirm then, James Roddick does work at this company? Only, I heard he might have . . . moved on.'

The receptionist sounds a bit confused now. 'No, no I don't think so. Definitely not, in fact. I saw him myself this morning.'

I don't say anything. My heart is still thumping. I wonder if the receptionist can hear it.

'Hello?' she says. 'Are you still there? Do you want to leave a message?'

'No. No thanks.'

I hang up.

I sit back down on my bed. I run my hand through my hair, then push my fists into my eyes so hard that I start to see light blotches when I take them away. I scroll through my phone to Edie's number, but I don't call. I just look at the numbers for ages, until they become meaningless lines and shapes.

I go back to my computer and type Edie Southwood into Google but I quickly see that none of the results are anything to do with her – it's all just random people on the Canadian electoral roll, kids, a road called Southwood Drive somewhere. I try Edith Southwood, but still nothing.

My first thought is that Edie Southwood doesn't even exist – she's made up the name, taken on a fake persona. But then I remember the way she clumsily reeled off that list of random letters before forlornly concluding that she didn't have an email address. Could it be possible that she just doesn't exist in the online world at all?

I reason that maybe Edie's name – made up or otherwise – doesn't matter right now anyway. That's not the point. The point right *now* is that James is alive. My father is alive. Not dead. And if he's alive, then why would Edie tell me he was dead? What could there possibly be in it for her? If there was a clear reason – if she'd got anything from me at all – then I would feel hoodwinked right now. Angry. But I just can't see any reason why someone would lie about this. I don't know who Edie Southwood really is, but I know I want to find out.

I decide I need to talk to her.

34

'Oh, hi!' she says when she opens the door. 'I hoped you'd come today. I can't wait to show you!'

She doesn't wait for me to say anything. She just turns and heads back into the flat. She leaves the door hanging open; I'm obviously supposed to follow her in, but I stay on the door-step, rooted to the spot. It feels weird that she should be acting so normally, so upbeat, even though I know there's no reason she should guess what's happened during the last hour. What I've found out. What I'm there for.

When she realises I haven't come inside, she turns back. She gives me a confused smile. 'Well, come on in then!' Then she sees my face. Her expression changes. 'What's the matter? What's happened? Is it Leon? Come inside and tell me.'

'No.' I take a step back away from the door. I suddenly wonder if it was a bad idea for me to come here alone. I haven't told anyone where I am.

Edie looks confused, worried. 'Anna? What's going on? What's happened? Please, tell me.'

'You've been lying to me.' My voice is flat, emotionless.

It's a simple statement of fact. I'm too confused to know how else to sound.

'What?'

'You've been lying, since we met. Every day. About everything. Who even *are* you?'

I'm still standing a good two metres away from her. I realise I'm poised like a cat, ready to run if I need to.

'Anna, *please*.' She runs her hand through her hair. She looks perplexed, pained even. I suppose her confusion is genuine. She can't know I've found out the truth.

'He's not dead!' My voice isn't so calm now. I can hear a definite wobble. 'My father isn't dead. Not dead at all! I've spoken to him! I've spoken to his work! Why would you lie? That's what I don't get – *why*?'

Edie doesn't say anything. She just blinks. Her hands are hanging down by her sides. 'What? What about James?' She looks stunned, like she's been given a slap.

'I've spoken to him,' I repeat. 'Today.'

Edie takes a step back into her hall, a step away from me. 'What? You're lying.'

'I spoke to him,' I say, trying to keep my voice steady. 'I spoke to him, and then I found him online and I spoke to his work and they saw him today. Very much alive. *Not dead*.'

Edie puts a hand out to steady herself against the wall. She's shaking her head. 'I don't understand, I don't understand. No. No. James is dead . . . he's . . .' She turns back to look at me again. She composes herself and stands upright again. 'Anna, I'm really sorry but I think someone's been having you on. Could it be Leon? Could this be some sick joke? James is dead, Anna. Your dad is dead.'

My head feels like it's spinning again. I feel like I don't know anything for sure. I can't trust anyone. Maybe they're all in this – Leon and Edie. And Mum and George and Sienna. It's all a joke. They're all setting me up for some kind of elaborate reality show to see what it takes to make me crack. In a minute some shiny-toothed TV presenter will step out from behind a bush and say, 'OK, that's a wrap. Wasn't she great, folks? Anna Roddick, everyone!'

I remember the voicemail that Dad – or whoever it was – left for me. That will still be there. Unless I imagined the whole thing, of course.

'Here.' I dial my voicemail number and set my phone to speaker. 'Listen to this.'

Neither of us moves while the message plays. When it's finished, Edie looks like she's been hit with a sack of bricks. She stumbles back towards the wall and sinks down until she's sitting on the floor in her hallway. Her knees are pulled up to her chin and she's just shaking her head and saying 'no' over and over again.

'They told me,' she says. Her voice sounds strange. 'They told me he was dead.'

I don't say anything. I just look at her sitting there, shaking her head. The realisation comes slowly. Things have shifted again. This whole situation is so weird, so slippery that what's true and what's a lie can flip and turn around in an instant. Edie may not be a liar. She might have been lied to herself. And if that really is what's happening here, then Edie is much more of a victim than I am. I got told a man I hadn't seen for

185

years – and didn't plan to see again – was dead. She got told the man she'd seen *every day* for the last eight years was dead.

That's much worse. That's pretty messed up.

Three minutes ago Edie was a manipulative liar, she was someone to be angry with, but more than that, she was someone to be wary of. Now though, she could be a victim, sitting there crying and shaking. I hate to say it but victim-Edie feels much more like the Edie I've got to know over the last few months than con-artist-Edie does. Innocent. Gullible. Naive. That fits with everything I know about her. She is the type of woman who could so easily be tricked.

There are still lots of unanswered questions. There's still too much that doesn't make sense. I'm still not sure if everything Edie's told me has been completely accurate or if she's been keeping back certain aspects of her story, but I no longer feel scared of her. I'm not ready to comfort her, to be friends again. But I am willing to talk to her.

I step over her and head to the kitchen. 'I'll make the tea.'

35

An hour later and we're sitting on opposite sides of the lounge, our hands curled around mugs of tea. Edie has made me play the voicemail message to her three times. She made me phone the advertising company again and listened to the – now slightly bemused – receptionist confirm that James had been seen alive and well that morning. She cried for twenty minutes straight. I just watched, waited. I still wasn't sure what was going on here. I just wanted the truth.

When the crying had been going on for a while, I said, 'So, you're telling me that you honestly believed James had died?'

'Yes!' she wailed. 'Yes!' and then dissolved into further sobs.

Now she seems to have calmed down a bit. She's sitting on her sagging old sofa, her legs tucked up underneath her. She's gazing vacantly into the middle of the room. I have no idea what she's thinking. I have no idea what I'm thinking, come to that. I don't say anything; I don't ask any questions. I just wait.

Eventually, she starts talking.

'We weren't . . . we weren't in a good place, relationshipwise. I told you, didn't I? I was staying in a B and B? When Marcus called me . . . I hadn't seen your father for . . .' She shakes her head. 'I don't know. Over a month.'

'That's a long time.'

'I know. He was . . . is . . . stubborn. When we used to fight at the beginning, I'd get fed up after a few days and try to call, or go and see him, and he'd treat me like . . . like some mad stalker. He'd tell me he never wanted to see me again, that I had to leave him alone. And then I started to realise that that's what I had to do. If I tried to push it, to pester him, to reason with him, it'd just push him further away. I realised that I just had to wait. Wait until he was ready. That's what I was doing when Marcus phoned – waiting. But then Marcus said he was dead . . .'

'What about a funeral? Didn't you ask about it? Didn't you want to go?'

I can't help but feel a bit impatient with her. How could she have let this happen?

Edie shook her head. 'Already happened, apparently. I missed it. No one thought to tell me. I was only his mad ex after all . . .' She does a short, hard laugh.

I frown, thinking back to our first meeting in The Last Drop. 'But didn't you tell me you went to it . . . you did a reading?'

Edie looks down into her mug. 'I was embarrassed, wasn't I? What kind of girlfriend doesn't get invited to her own boyfriend's funeral? It was the same with that necklace. Remember that little cross I gave you?'

I remember the red velvet box. The randomness of it all when I didn't have any explanation for what it was or why he'd left it to me.

'That was never his. I bought it from the market. I just wanted to have something to give you. I didn't think you'd agree to meet me otherwise. But I didn't have anything. He never gave me anything. I assumed he'd left me with nothing.'

I close my eyes for a minute, trying to take this in. 'But how . . . how could he pull it off? He couldn't have pretended to be dead to everyone, surely? He's still going to work! And why turn up now, why ring me and tell me?'

'It would've been easy enough. He had his friends; I had . . . well, I had no one. He went out drinking after work, went into town. Skiing weekends. I didn't go. He could tell his friends to go along with it, or not tell them anything. I never saw them anyway. I'm guessing . . . I'm only guessing . . . but I reckon the whole thing was only ever going to be a temporary plan.'

I raise one eyebrow. 'A temporary death?'

She laughs, but it's not a real laugh. 'I know. I know. Look, Anna, the truth is, when James and I were "off", when we'd had a row and he wouldn't talk to me, the way he'd act – like I'd never existed at all – would make me come over all desperate. I'm guessing you've worked this out by now but I don't exactly have a lot going on in my life. James was it. James was everything. When he took that away from me – took himself away from me – it made me act kind of . . . eccentric. I would ring more than I should have, go over too much.' She shakes her head and does another not-laughing laugh. 'I'd go to his work. I'd wait for him . . . god. Pathetic.'

It's weird but something about this bit makes me warm to her again. Although I do realise that what she's telling me is clear evidence that she's a few rungs short of a ladder, something about the total honesty of it all makes me think she can't be lying. This *can't* be one big con. It just doesn't feel like that. Edie is definitely sad, and probably a bit mad, but I just can't believe that anything about her is really *bad*.

'He'd be cruel at those times,' she goes on. 'He'd treat me like I was crazy – that's what he'd tell people too. And the more he did that, the more he shut me out, the more I'd *act* crazy. I don't know. Maybe I was crazy. But then we'd get back together. We'd put the whole thing behind us. He'd be lovely again and say we'd never fight again and that I had nothing to worry about. And that would be it. Until the next time . . . I was stupid. *Stupid*. Why did I keep going back?'

'Why *did* you keep going back?'

Edie pauses for a very long time. 'I don't know,' she says eventually.

I rub my eyes with my index fingers. I'm tired. This is tiring. 'So . . . I still don't get why he's called me?'

Edie thinks, chewing on her lip. Her eyes are narrowed as she stares at the empty space in the middle of the room. 'No . . . it's strange. I can only think that it's because he's found out somehow . . . that we've become . . . that we've met. He wouldn't like that. He'll still think of you as "his". He was like that.'

I make a kind of involuntarily snorting noise at the idea that he could lay any kind of claim to me after all this time, after he was the one who walked out on us.

'James was always very particular about what was his,' Edie explains. '*His* friends, *his* work. His things. He kept them very separate. He even had his own rooms in the house. Rooms that I couldn't go in.'

I shake my head. 'He sounds mental.'

Edie shrugs. 'Maybe. Maybe we both are. But something I'm sure of now is that James is not a very nice man. I'm sorry to say it, I know he'll always be your father, but he was cruel to me, Anna. Cruel and cold and controlling. And, in a way, I'm glad he's done this, done this horrible trick on me. Because it's given me time to think about things, to look at things properly. I know now that he was never right for me but I've needed this time away to realise it. And, what's more, it's shown me what he's really like. Just how far he's willing to go to have things his own way.'

'I have to go.' I stand up. I know it sounds abrupt but I'm exhausted. I just don't want to be here any more. I don't want to listen any more or think any more.

Edie blinks. 'Oh. OK. Yes.'

'What will you do now?' I ask.

'Now?'

'Now you know he's not dead.'

Edie looks around her. She shrugs. 'Nothing, I suppose. Carry on as I was. In a way, nothing's changed. He's still dead to me.'

'Don't you want to speak to him? To get an explanation?'

Edie shakes her head. 'No. No. What would be the point? He'll just tell me I'm crazy and that I drove him to it. I don't need to hear that. I don't need that explanation.'

As soon as I've left Edie's place to head home I pull out my phone. I find the number that called me earlier and hit the call button.

Edie might not want to hear an explanation, but I do.

36

'Anna?'

'She says you lied to her. She says you pretended to be dead.'

'Oh, I'm sure she did.' He laughs a cold laugh. I don't like the sound of it. I don't like the sound of him. 'She's come up with some rubbish in her time but this little stunt takes the cake.' He sighs a weary sigh, like he's finding this whole situation a terrible drag. 'Listen to me, Anna. Edie's . . . well, she's a nightmare, to be honest. My mate on the council down there near you said he thought he'd seen you together, so I got him to do some digging through the files and he confirmed that she'd parked herself down on the coast. God knows why. To get her claws into you, I suppose. To use you to get to me. She's a total lun—'

'Yeah, a lunatic. You said that bit. She says that your colleague phoned her and told her you were dead. Marcus.'

'Oh, for goodness' sake. It was just some throwaway comment! – "Is James there?" "No he's out." "Is James there?" "No, he's dead" – you know, a joke.'

I don't say anything. Sounds like a weird kind of joke to me.

He sighs again. It annoys me when he does that. 'Listen, Anna. The fact is –' He's cut off by someone talking to him in the background. A woman. I hear him muffle the handset but I can still hear what he says to her. 'There in a minute, sweetie. Just got to deal with this.' That annoys me even more. I am something to be dealt with. Just like Edie was something to be dealt with.

'Listen, Anna,' he says again. 'Edie's not that stable and not that bright. Just stay away from her, OK?'

Suddenly I've had enough of him. Who does he think he is, rocking up after all this time, telling me what to do and who to talk to? His tone is almost unbearable.

I hang up.

It's the next morning when I remember the text Edie sent me the day before, before our confrontation. The text about Leon and the answer to all my problems.

I type out a reply:

You never showed me what you were going to show me.
About Leon.

She replies at once.

No. I just remembered that. I still think you should see it,
whatever you think of me. It might help you.

I write three words back.

I'll come tonight.

Edie opens the door, tentatively, when I call round straight from school. She looks exhausted. Her cheeks are puffy. Her eyes are swollen. I get the feeling she hasn't slept since I last saw her.

'Anna,' she says quietly.

I step inside. 'How's it going?'

Edie nods slowly. 'OK. OK.'

I follow her into the flat. She makes us drinks and we take a seat in the lounge. Neither of us mentions the day before, but we're being careful with each other. Things are a long way from normal.

'Thanks for coming over.'

'It's OK.' I look around the room a bit. Our cups from the day before are still on the window sill. I wonder if Edie slept last night, if she went to work today.

The clock is ticking loudly. A car drives past outside. 'So . . .'

'Yes. So . . .'

I don't say anything. I don't really feel like small talk. I want her to get on with it.

'I'll go and get it.' Edie goes to her bedroom and comes back a few seconds later carrying a book and a magazine. 'I was in the newsagents the other day, just looking for a magazine to read in my lunch break, when I saw this – and I recognised it from that one Leon showed you on the beach that time. You know, when he was all strutting about, boasting about his short story being published?' She holds the magazine out. I definitely recognise the cover – it's got some weird sculpture on the front. I don't know what it's supposed to be but to me it looks like an enormous grey bum.

I peer at it. 'So . . . is that the exact same edition?'

Edie nods. 'Yes. It's only quarterly. More of an anthology than a magazine really, it seems. So for a minute I thought, blimey, maybe the little toe rag was right to be pleased with himself after all. It certainly looks the part – shiny cover, proper thick pages. All that. Anyway, I flicked through, just out of curiosity really, and I found his little story. "The Witch's Hour", it's called. I don't know if you ever bothered reading it?'

I pull a face and shake my head.

'From what you've told me about Leon and his "creative writing", I was bracing myself for some major rubbish. Just from seeing the boy a couple of times myself, I thought I knew the type – flouncy descriptions, why use two words when twenty will do, all that sort of thing. But then when I started reading it, it wasn't like that at all. I mean, I'm no literary critic but I do like a good book – and not just the trashy ones either – and I could see that this was snappy and smart and funny. It was *good*.'

'Really?' I sound irritated because I am. Partly to find out that maybe Leon does indeed have the talent he's so fond of telling me about, but also because I don't know why Edie would think I'd want to hear about it.

Edie nods. 'Really. So I read on. And I got quite into it, because it was good –'

'Yeah. You said.' I sigh and look out of the window. Why is she telling me this?

'Let me finish. But then I got to a bit and I thought, *hang on*. And I thought, this is familiar. And then I read some more and I thought, this is *very* familiar. So I buy the thing – because by this point the old boy behind the counter is giving me the evil eye – and then later that night, when I got home, I rummaged through some boxes and I found this.' She holds up a book. It's quite slim, with a blue front cover. She passes it to me. 'I don't know if you've heard of the author, he's not massively famous, but he is quite well thought of. Literary, you know. High-brow.'

I look at the name written in small white capitals typed along the bottom of the cover. I smile. HENRY MCCAIN.

'Yeah. I've heard of him. Likes a whisky, I've heard.' I get an image of him knocking back the drinks that night in the basement of The Centipede, that scornful look in his eye as Leon tried so desperately to impress him.

'Well, that little book you're holding is one of his first short story collections. Some of his very earliest stuff is in there, stuff he did at college, I think. I mean, it's nowhere near as well known as his novels, the work he does these days, but I was quite into short stories for a while – short stories are the insomniac's best friend, you know – and I read that collection to death. Certainly know them all well enough to spot one when it turns up in a magazine thirty years after it was originally published, under the new name of Leon Jakes-Field.'

I look from the magazine to the book and back again.

'You mean, Leon copied his story out of a book? Out of a book that Henry McCain wrote?'

Edie nods, her eyes shining. 'That's exactly what I mean. Look for yourself. I've folded over the corner.'

I turn to the page Edie's marked in the book and then find the story in the magazine and compare them side by side. It's exactly as she says. A carbon copy. Henry McCain's original has a different title – 'Midnight Sun' – but everything else is the same.

I put the stories down on my lap. 'He's such a little cheat!' I shake my head, almost in disbelief. But I can believe it really. This kind of trick has Leon written all over it.

Edie nods. 'Yep. Shameless, barefaced copying.'

I just shake my head again and laugh and look back down at the two identical stories.

'So, there you have it,' Edie says, leaning back in her chair. 'He's got something on you, sure. But now you've got something on him. You're even. They cancel each other out. Which means, now he's got nothing.'

I think about this for a minute. 'Yeah, but . . . I'm not sure copying a little story is quite the same as . . .'

'Actual bodily harm on a small boy?'

I wince.

'Maybe not to an outsider, but you've got think about how important this is to Leon. I would be willing to bet that he'd rather people found out he'd Actual Bodily Harmed a thousand people than have people realise he's a talentless little twerp whose one and only success came from a story he copied from someone else.'

I nod slowly. She has a point. Ever since the story was published Leon has been banging about it on his blog, talking about it in his little creative writing club. It's been his defining work.

I smile. 'Well done for spotting it. A bloody good find.'

Edie grins. 'All you've got to do now is break the good news to him and put this whole stupid mess to bed.'

37

To say I'm nervous about letting Leon know what I've found is an understatement – I don't like confrontation at the best of times and this one has the potential to be very nasty but I know I need to get it out of the way sooner rather than later. Like Edie says, I just want to put this whole stupid mess to bed.

I get an opportunity two days after Edie showed me his story, when I see him walking out of school down the back road that leads to the high street. I've had both the magazine and Edie's copy of Henry McCain's book in my bag since she gave them to me, just in case Leon tries to flat-out deny what he's done and I need to produce proof.

This is a conversation that we need to have away from the crowds of kids from school who are all swarming up to the bus stop on the main road, so I follow him for a while as he turns onto the high street and walks down the road. After about five minutes he ducks into a shop on the corner, and when he emerges a few minutes later with a bottle of mineral water, I'm there to greet him.

'Good afternoon, Anna,' he says, with a little nod and an amused smile. 'What a delightful surprise.'

I don't return the smile. 'We need to talk.'

'A wonderful idea.' He's still smirking. 'How I love to talk.'

'Over here.' I lead him to a bench at the edge of the dog-walkers' field, just tucked away enough to stop any unwanted eavesdroppers.

He raises his eyebrows slightly but doesn't argue. 'Charmingly mysterious.' He sits down and leans back, stretching his arm out along the backrest. 'So. How are you, Anna?'

I ignore the question. 'This has to stop.'

'I'm sorry?' There is the tiniest curl at his lip. He looks pleased with himself. He always looks pleased with himself.

I look at him. I look hard and for longer than I'm really comfortable with. I need to be strong and firm and definite. 'You know,' I say eventually. 'We're not together. We're not even friends. You can't keep pretending you're going to drop me in it, just to make me do what you want. You can't.'

The sneer is still there. 'Pretending?' he says in a light, sing-song voice.

I keep looking. Staring him right in the eye. 'Yes. You won't say anything. You can't. Because if you do, if you tell anyone what happened – what you made it look like happened – with Shay Bradstock then I will tell everyone all about how your little story in *Pencil* is a word-for-word copy of "Midnight Sun" by Henry McCain. I'll tell them and I'll show them and then *everyone* will know what an absolute fraud you are.'

The sly smile on Leon's face disappears immediately. His features seem frozen for a moment, but then his eyes narrow and fix on mine. I don't let myself look away.

I expect him to deny it, to tell me I'm talking rubbish or that he has no idea what I'm on about, all that sort of thing. But he doesn't.

Instead he leans in close to me. He puts his hand on my knee. I try to jerk it away, but he just tightens his grip. He puts his head close to mine. I think he's going to kiss me again, like that time in the science corridor. I'm sure anyone who's watching would think that too – two teenage lovebirds on a bench after school. The thought makes me feel sick. He doesn't kiss me, though. He just starts to speak, in a low monotone. He doesn't sound angry, or panicked. His voice has no expression at all.

'You won't, Anna. You won't tell anyone anything. Because if you do, your little bit of rough-and-tumble with the Bradstock boy will be the least of your worries. If you do anything – *anything* – out of line, I will get you. I will get you back. My revenge will be ten-fold. Do you understand? Your life will not be worth living.'

As he's been speaking, his fingers have been digging further and further into my knee. It feels more like a bite than a grip. Then he pulls away suddenly. He stands up, straightens the lapels on his blazer and gives me a little nod. 'Goodbye, Anna.' He turns and strides away.

I stay on the bench. I can't move. My heart is smashing against my rib cage but I feel frozen to the spot. I look down at my knee. There are four red indentations were Leon had his hand. That really happened.

I watch a police car pull into the bus stop. There are two policemen inside. The passenger door opens and one gets out. He starts to walk along the pavement in my direction and I sit up a little straighter. He's going to ask me if I'm OK, if that boy was bothering me. I need to decide what my answer's going to be. Shall I tell him? Could I really report Leon to the police?

But the policeman doesn't turn and walk towards my bench. He just keeps walking along the pavement towards the shop. He goes inside and a few minutes later he comes out with a four-cheese ravioli ready-meal and an eight-pack of Kit-Kats. He walks back to the car, climbs in and drives away.

I start laughing – actually laughing out loud. There I was, thinking a nice policeman was going to come along and save me from my troubles when all he was doing was buying a four-cheese ravioli and some Kit-Kats. It just seems so funny! Doesn't it?

But then I realise there are tears, running down cheeks and dripping off my chin, and I don't think they're tears of laughter.

Oh god, not this again. Not this mad laughing. I'm mad.

I'm mad and I'm in trouble and I'm totally out of options.

38

I think about telling Edie about what happened but something stops me. I guess I feel that there's been enough drama between us for one week. I just want to let things lie for a while, see if we can get things back on an even keel. And more to the point, there's really nothing she can do now. It was good to get the whole Shay story off my chest and, fair play to Edie, she's never made me feel like a monster about it. She's been great really. But she was so pleased with herself for spotting Leon's plagiarism – and quite right too, it was a hell of a hand to be able to play – but the fact of the matter is, I don't think it was enough.

As I make my way home after my failed attempt at scaring Leon off, I try to make sense of what he said, and what would happen if I did tell people the truth about his story. The thing is, the major problem with the whole plan, is that it was only ever going to work as a threat. The power of the thing came from the promise of what was to come if Leon didn't back down. Where it fell apart is where I played out what would happen if I did actually go ahead and tell everyone what he'd done.

If I did do that, if I did make it public knowledge that he was a cheat and a liar, then there would be some satisfying repercussions, sure – the magazine would no doubt pull his story, he'd be a joke in his precious 'literary community' – but none of these things would actually help me. And more to the point, things for me would be worse than ever. His first revenge move would of course be to spread the story – and the video – of what I did to Shay, so things would already look pretty bad for me. But on top of that, I reckon there's a good chance he'd follow through with whatever else he was planning to do to me, whatever he had in mind to make my life 'not worth living'. So, following things to their logical conclusion, the discovery of Leon's fraud had got me precisely nowhere.

The threat hadn't worked. I'm back to square one. Leon has all the power.

I don't sleep well that night. The couple of hours I do manage are filled with unsettling dreams – Leon leaning in close to whisper into my ear, then his tongue darting out like a lizard's to lick my face. Edie sitting in a crumpled heap on her doorstep, sobbing into her *Pride and Prejudice* dress. The next day at school, I'm tired and grumpy. I know I'm not being good company.

I'm sitting with George in our tutor room waiting for afternoon registration and he's talking about this boy in our year called Findlay Lawson, who's a bit of a joke, always getting into trouble for stupid things – getting locked out of the changing room in his pants, spilling pig's guts all over himself in biology, that kind of thing. George is telling me some long-winded and animated story about how a bunch of boys in Findlay's Spanish class managed to convince him that one of their exchange partners was in love with him, and gave him a list of random gifts to present her with that were supposedly signs of respect in Spanish culture, one of which apparently included a live sheep. So as we speak Findlay is making his way out of school in disgrace, ordered to return the sheep to the farm where he found it, having thoroughly freaked out the nice Spanish girl he was trying to impress.

Just as George reaches the end of the story, Sienna bounds into the classroom. 'Oh my god, oh my god, *so* funny! I've just bumped into that idiot Findlay Lawson and you will absolutely never guess what he had with him!'

I stand up so abruptly that I knock my chair over. 'A sheep! A stupid fucking sheep!' I grab my bag and rush out of the classroom, leaving George and Sienna staring after me, mouths open in surprise.

I regret my irrational outburst as soon as I'm out in the corridor. I'm basically only annoyed at them for being normal and happy and carefree when I am caught up in this nightmare of my own making and that makes no sense at all. And I know that the one thing that is definitely not going to help me at all is alienating the few people in my life who are not causing me one massive headache. I decide to do a quick circuit of the corridor to pull myself together then head back to apologise. But as I turn the corner that leads to the art department, I see Leon walking towards me.

I panic. I do the only thing I can think of, which is an abrupt about-turn and walking quickly in the opposite direction.

'Anna!' he calls. 'Hi there, Anna!'

I pretend not to hear. I walk quickly, aiming to get back to the safety of the tutor room as quickly as possible but he just speeds up too. He catches me up. Then he overtakes and steps out in front of me, blocking my path.

'Hey, no need to hide from me!' He flashes me a sinister smile.

I don't reply. I just look at him. If I don't give him anything to bounce off, maybe he'll get bored and move aside.

'You're looking nice today.' He's still doing the smile. It's a smile that says, 'I'm winning. I will win this game.'

I still don't say anything. I just spin around and start walking in the opposite direction again, back towards the art department.

'Wait!' Leon reaches out and grabs my arm. I try to shake him off but he grips tighter. I notice a girl from a few years below looking at us. I'm tempted to shout, to let everyone know that Leon is bothering me, but my rational side tells me that's not a good idea. Even if it gets Leon to back off right now, he'll be back worse than ever soon enough. Instead, I just freeze. I don't look at him. I'm still facing the opposite direction. Leon is talking to the back of my head.

'Listen. I'm not going to hurt you. I just need you to do me a favour.'

39

I don't move. I don't speak.

'I've left my bag in the PE department . . . in the cone cupboard,' he goes on. 'You couldn't do a fella a favour and fetch it for me, could you?'

I turn to face him now. I look at him through narrowed eyes. I'm trying to work out what his game is here. The PE department is just around the corner from where we're standing. It wouldn't take him any more than thirty seconds to get to the cone cupboard. There is absolutely no reason for him to ask me to do it. Or rather, there is a reason and that reason is that he wants to mess with me. This is just a mind-game. This is how Leon wants to demonstrate his control over me, to show me that I am his.

I weigh up my options. I could refuse but then I can't predict what will happen next. I can't predict what will happen next if I do fetch it either, of course, but it feels safer. I'll just do this now, and buy myself some time. Running some pointless errand is annoying and I hate the satisfaction it will give Leon when he realises he can use me as his skivvy, but when I compare it to all the things he could be making me do . . . well, it could be worse.

I still don't say anything to Leon. I just wriggle my arm free of his grasp, shoot him one last glare, then head for the PE department.

The cone cupboard is big inside – more of a room than a cupboard really, although it doesn't have any windows. Along one wall are crash mats and gym mats, piled high like luxury beds. Along the other side is all sorts of games equipment – orange cones, footballs, hula hoops. I have no idea what Leon would have been doing in the cupboard, or why his bag should be in there at all, but then I don't think this is really about Leon absent-mindedly leaving his belongings lying around.

Leon hasn't given me any indication of where in the cupboard his bag might be, but as I'm sure that he's aiming to make this as awkward as possible for me, to make sure I know how much power he has over me, I expect that he will have hidden it somewhere, or maybe put it up high, so I'll have to scramble over mats and goal frames and buckets of netball bibs to get to it.

I push the door open and squint, my eyes taking a few seconds to get used to the dim light. I'm surprised to spot Leon's leather satchel straight away, just sitting there on top of a pile of crash mats in the far corner of the room.

There are all sorts of background noises around – people shouting, kids and teachers shuffling along the corridor outside, doors slamming – but as I make my way across the room to Leon's bag, I get the feeling that there's a noise coming from inside the cupboard itself. It sounds like a girl trying to stifle giggles, like someone trying not to be seen. I look back towards the door to see if some annoying Year Seven has followed me in, but everything seems still.

I decide it must've come from outside after all and continue on my mission to the far corner. Then as I take a side-step to avoid the base of a portable basketball hoop, a movement to my left catches my eye. I jerk my head round and look down to find that I'm looking directly at Callum Steward and Madison Porter.

'Oh!' I say, surprised.

They're sitting in the space between two towers of crash mats. Callum is leaning against the wall. One arm is draped around Madison's shoulders, the other is resting on his knee. In his hand there's a bottle of vodka. It's almost empty.

'All right?' he says, looking up at me dopily.

'Yeah. I just need to . . .' I gesture towards Leon's bag.

'Just need to what?' Callum says.

'Get something.'

'What you stood there for, then? Get on with it.'

Madison giggles and buries her head in Callum's shoulder. Then she sits up again and takes the bottle from him. She takes a long swig.

I dart forwards into the corner of the room, grab Leon's bag from the top of the mats. Clutching it to my chest I make for the door.

'Oi, Anna,' Madison calls.

I turn to look at her. She holds one finger up to her lips, staring at me hard the whole time. The universal sign for silence. She needn't have bothered. I've got enough problems of my own; I hardly need to get involved in any more awkward situations.

I nod once, and step out into the corridor, slamming the door behind me.

As I head down the corridor, Leon's bag still in my arms like a sack of coal, I pass Mr Rutland – head of PE, ex-army, all round tough guy – striding in the opposite direction. I pause for a moment to see where he's going in such a hurry, and see him head straight for the cone cupboard.

I hang around just long enough to hear him shout, 'Right, you two. On your feet. Now! And give me that!'

I shake my head gently and roll my eyes. They were asking for it really.

I decide not to stick around to see Callum and Madison get marched into Rutland's office. I head back down the corridor towards the tutor room to find Leon where I left him. I thrust the satchel into his stomach, accompanied by my best death stare.

'Thank you so much, Anna!' he calls after me. 'You really are most obliging!'

40

The next day, I'm woken by the doorbell. I check my watch. It's not even seven yet – surely even Sienna can't think this is acceptable? I pull a hoody on over my pyjamas and head downstairs. I open the front door and realise I'm wrong – Sienna does apparently think this is acceptable.

'Sienna! For Christ's sake – '

'Anna!' she says, stepping into the hallway. 'You absolute loon! What did you do that for?'

I just look at her. 'What?'

'Why did you get Rutland to go and ambush Stewport like that?' Her eyes are gleaming. She's obviously delighted with whatever drama she's come to report.

'What?' I say again, but already I'm starting to fit the pieces together. It's all totally obvious, really.

'Rutland caught Callum and Madison having a lunchtime party and now they've both been suspended and everyone's saying that you sent Rutland in to bust them and Madison is saying she's going to put dog shit through your letterbox!'

I groan. 'For god's sake . . .' I slump down at the kitchen table. Sienna sits opposite me and rests her chin on her knuckles.

'So!' she says. 'Why did you do it then, you nutter?'

'I didn't!' It comes out as a shout and Sienna blinks. 'I didn't,' I say again in a more reasonable tone.

Sienna frowns and twirls a strand of her hair around her finger. 'But they're saying – Callum, Madison, everyone – that you walked in on them, took one look at them, then scuttled right off to summon Rutland.'

I sigh. 'I didn't. I didn't scuttle. I didn't summon. I just went in and went out again. Rutland was already on his way when I left.'

'Oh. Well, that's not what everyone's saying.' Sienna frowns, obviously put out that her version of the story is being questioned. 'Anyway, I expect you'll still get the dog shit through your letterbox,' she adds brightly.

On the way to school I reassure myself with the knowledge that if Callum and Madison have been suspended, at least I won't have to face them.

This turns out to be wishful thinking.

Over the course of the day, everyone in Callum and Madison's group and plenty of other people in the year make a special effort to seek me out so they can ask me over and over why I grassed Stewport up and what my problem is and if I think I'm better than everyone. I get so used to protesting my innocence that I start saying, 'I didn't, OK?' before each new visitor has even announced their grievances.

Then, as I'm making my way up the field to head for home that afternoon, Madison herself steps out from the trees.

I'm more than a little tempted to blank her but I know that's likely to get me in even more trouble. I decide my best bet is to just be nice, to act as normal as possible and, if given the opportunity, to state my case.

'Hi,' I say, as brightly as possible.

'Happy are you, then?' She's smoking a cigarette. She finishes it and stubs it out on a tree.

'I know what you think I did, but that's not what happened. I didn't say anything. Seriously, Madison. I was just –'

'Getting your bag – yeah, whatever. Like why would you leave your bag in there? That doesn't even make any sense.'

'I didn't. I *didn't* leave my bag then.' I can't hide the frustration in my voice, and this riles her.

She takes a step forward. Her face is right up close to mine. 'Don't bullshit me, Roddick. Rutland was there right after you, like, the second you left, you know? He was straight on the phone to our parents and now I'm in serious shit with my old man. Cal's too freaked out to even come near my house any more. And it's all your fault. So what is it, Anna? What *is* your problem? Are you trying to start something or what?'

I take a step back from her. Starting something – starting anything – is about the last thing I want right now.

'Seriously. I didn't say anything. I didn't say a word about the drinking, about anything. To anyone. Why would I?'

Madison just keeps staring at me, her eyes narrowed. 'Because you're a pathetic little freak. But I'll tell you something Anna Roddick, I've got a lot more friends than you in that place.' She points towards the school. 'And you piss *me* off, you piss *them* off. So you just made yourself a whole load of enemies. Well done. Well *done*.'

Part of me does want to argue – to convince her of my innocence, of the truth – but a bigger part just wants to not be standing here having this confrontation. In the end, I sigh and turn, and walk away.

'This is not the end of this conversation, Roddick!' she shouts after me.

When I get home, I'm in a seriously foul mood.

Madison's right. She has got a lot of friends and if she decides to set them on me, in one single move I will have made an enemy out of half of Year Eleven. Leon's been clever. Rather than just tormenting me himself, he's set things up so that a whole army of Stewport supporters will do his dirty work for him. It's a typical Leon move.

The worst part of all of it though, the part that's really bugging me, is that I don't know what Leon has planned next. Today has been difficult and stressful and frustrating, but what if he decides to take things up a level? What if things get darker? What if he gets more . . . dangerous?

As I head into the kitchen to get a drink, I can hear Mum on the phone in her study. Whatever she's talking about clearly isn't going well.

'Of *course* it's big for the department but it was also big for me. You know I needed this, Jonathan, so don't give me all that "in this together" crap. You're a backstabbing bastard, it's as simple as that.'

I guess Mum then hangs up on Jonathan the backstabbing bastard, because I hear the door to her study being flung open, and her footsteps stomping down the stairs.

As she comes into the kitchen, she trips over a pair of her own shoes that are lying in the doorway. She swears and walks straight past me without saying hello, and puts a plate and a mug from the sideboard into the sink. 'This place is a pigsty. Clear it up, will you?'

I jerk my head up and look at her. I know she's only in a bad mood because of whatever that phone call was about but this time I don't care. So what if she's had a bad day? So have I. And I've had enough of being her punchbag.

'Why don't *you* clear it up? It's mostly yours anyway. Why don't *you* do something for a change?'

Mum spins around and glares at me. She appears calm on the outside but there's a dishcloth in her hands that she's twisting round and round into a thick rope. 'Why don't I do something? What do you think I do every day? Do you think I do this for fun? Do you think I live this *life* for fun? Do you think I like being strung along for weeks on end by self-satisfied "professors" whose research isn't even half as developed as mine? Do you think I like working sixteen-hour days on a project just to get it pulled at the last minute?'

I'm not going to shout. That's what she wants. She wants me to shout so she can be the calm, collected one, sneering at me as I lose my temper. I just look down and, deliberately nonchalantly, turn the page of my magazine. 'Get a different job then.'

I don't look up to see the look on her face but I know that will have surprised her. This is not the kind of thing I say to my mum.

'You little cow,' she hisses eventually. 'You can be a right little cow, you know that?'

I do shout then. I stand up and throw the magazine aside. 'Yeah? Well, so can you.'

Mum pushes past me and stamps back up the stairs to her study, slamming the door shut behind her. I stay where I am for a minute, breathing hard. Then I go to my room, throw a few random items – my phone, a hairbrush, a book – into a bag, and I leave the house.

41

I give Edie a rundown of the events of the last forty-eight hours in one highly charged, shouted rant, marching up and down her lounge, throwing my hands in the air at the key points to make sure she knows exactly how awful and terrible and incredibly *unfair* everything has been. In the drama queen stakes, I know I'm giving even Sienna a run for her money.

I tell Edie everything – Leon's furious response to the suggestion I might reveal his plagiarism, his threats, his cone cupboard stunt, all the idiots at school, moronic Madison and then Mum. I finish on my row with my cold, unfeeling mum.

'Oh, love,' Edie says, pulling me into a hug. 'What a rough old run of it, eh? Poor old sausage. Of course you can stay here for a couple of days. You'll have to sleep on the sofa again though I'm afraid, for the time-being anyway. Still need to sort that back room out!'

'That's fine. Wherever's fine. I'll just stay for one night anyway. I'll go home tomorrow, to sort things out with Mum ... to face ... everything ...' The thought of facing anything at all makes me feel exhausted. I rub my face with my hands. When I take them away, Edie's looking at me, her head on one side.

'Poor old sausage,' she says again. 'Poor love. You stay here for just as long as you like. Think of it as a holiday. Think of me as your protector!' She stands with her hands on her hips and her chest puffed out and I laugh, even though nothing really seems that funny, because it feels like the right thing to do.

Edie makes me a comforting dinner of chicken and mushroom pie, mashed potato and chocolate cake and prattles away about the fudge shop and how Isaac is giving her driving lessons in the delivery van. I'm not sure that's entirely legal but I guess it's a good thing that she has a project to focus on. It seems like she's getting back to normal since the whole bombshell of the not-actually-dead dad news. I'm aware that I've only said about two words during the whole time we've been eating but I figure that's often the way things are with me and Edie.

That is until she says, 'You're very quiet, love. And you look pale too. Do you feel OK?'

Now she's said it I realise that I do feel a bit rough. I don't have any symptoms as such, but I feel completely drained. Maybe it's the stress of the day, or maybe I am coming down with something. I shrug. 'I've felt better.'

Edie rushes into action at once, laying out a duvet on the sofa and making me a hot water bottle.

'Here,' she directs. 'You get comfy here and I'll make you some honey and lemon.'

I've never really liked honey but I can't be bothered to say anything. I just lie on my back staring at the telly but not really watching it while Edie fusses about in the kitchen.

'The lemons look a bit past it, I'm afraid. Best pop out for some more.'

'No, it's OK. I don't need them.'

'It's no trouble, love. I'll get you some flu stuff while I'm at it. You just sit tight here. Promise me you won't move a muscle?'

'Promise,' I mumble. The idea of moving anywhere doesn't really appeal right now.

'I'll get you something for breakfast too. What do you fancy? Poached eggs? Your favourite?'

I nod again, but I don't really care. I'm too tired. I just want her to be quiet so I can go to sleep.

I think I must have fallen asleep almost as soon as Edie leaves the flat. I'm only vaguely aware of her coming back later and putting a glass of water by the side of the sofa. Then the door to the lounge closes and I suppose she must be going to bed herself.

My phone rings in the middle of the night. Confused, I ignore it and look at my watch.

I see it's not the middle of the night at all. It's past nine o'clock in the morning. Alarmed, I try to sit up quickly, but I feel like I've been hit by a tractor. I scramble around next to the sofa to look at my phone. I have three missed calls from Sienna, no doubt wondering why I'm not at school. I've been asleep for nearly twelve hours but I still feel horrendous.

'Ah, you're awake, sleepyhead.' Edie appears in the doorway to the lounge.

'I'm late for school . . .' I try to prop myself up but I only manage to get halfway before sinking back down into the cushions.

'I think you'd best have a duvet day, don't you?' She hands me a hot mug. It's the honey and lemon she promised me last night.

'You found the lemons . . .'

'Yeah . . . You were dozing by the time I got back though! I didn't want to disturb you.'

'Sorry,' I mumble. 'Just so tired . . .'

'It's probably a virus. With all this stress your defences are down. Just relax today. You can lie there, under that duvet, and watch all the daytime rubbish on the telly.'

'Should I go home? I should go home . . .'

Edie crouches down and takes my hand in hers. 'Anna, love. Stop struggling. Stop trying to fight it. You're ill. Just stay there. Relax. It's my day off today and I can keep you fed and watered. I know your mum gets busy with work so . . .'

Edie doesn't finish the sentence but I know what she wants to say is she doesn't think Mum will be that interested in looking after me, and she's right.

The truth is that there is unlikely to be any real food in the house and even if there is, I have almost no chance of Mum bringing it to me or even getting me a glass of water. At any rate, I really can't face the trek in the freezing drizzle. Staying right here, in this warm duvet, with Edie waiting on me, seems the perfect option right now.

I barely move all day apart from three toilet trips, all of which feel like forty-mile hikes.

Edie brings me poached eggs for breakfast as promised, but I can't really face them. At some point in the afternoon she brings me a bowl of chicken soup, and I manage to eat half. Edie chats to me at various points in the day. She shows me articles from her magazine and reads me snippets. She puts the telly on for me and searches around for something I might

219

like. I can't be bothered with any of it. I barely move my head. Eventually she seems to get bored of me and disappears to do some 'tidying and other bits and pieces in another room'. I'm glad of the quiet when she's gone.

A few hours later, I look at my phone. It's nearly out of battery. I have five missed calls from Sienna and a text. Nothing from Mum though. I doubt she's noticed I've gone.

I read Sienna's text.

> *Where are you?? Guess what's funny –*
> *Leon's moving to Africa!*

I frown. The message makes no sense. My phone beeps once then switches itself off. Out of battery. I put it down by the side of me, and shuffle myself into a sitting position. Edie must have heard me stirring because she appears.

'How are you, love?' She stands over me, concerned. 'You've been asleep for nearly twenty-four hours, on and off. Do you feel any better for it?'

I do a few circles with my shoulders and stretch my arms above my head. 'Yeah, I suppose. Just a bit gross. I really should go home.'

Edie nods thoughtfully. 'Why don't I run you a bath? See how you feel then.'

I soak in the bath for well over half an hour, and afterwards I do feel better. I climb back into my crumpled clothes and wish I had something fresh to wear.

I slowly pack my things into my bag. 'Thanks, Edie. Seriously. For the food and everything. Sorry I've taken over your living room for so long.'

Edie's frowning, she still looks concerned. 'I don't think you should be going yet, to be honest, love. You still look very pale.'

I shake my head. 'Mum will start to worry . . .'

Edie lets out a kind of snorting noise. 'Doubt it.'

I'm surprised. Edie isn't one for scorn or sarcasm – if anything I sometimes find her a little too earnest – and I've definitely never heard her say a word against my mother, even when I've been laying into her pretty hard myself.

Edie sees my expression. 'Sorry, Anna. I know she's your mum but I do worry that she's so busy with her work. The last thing I want is for you is to get worse and there not be anyone to call a doctor.'

I think she's getting a bit carried away now. It's a bit of flu, not bubonic plague. 'I'll be fine. I feel better now.'

Edie nods. 'OK. Just have a quick cup of tea. Get something hot inside you before you head out into the cold.'

I nod and sink down onto the sofa. Edie chats away about something to do with the shop and a delivery she's expecting tomorrow while I sip my tea but I have a growing sense that I'm not really in the room. I feel like there's a thick fog around my head, a barrier between me and the real world. I lean backwards, my head lolling to one side.

'Are you OK, Anna?' Edie says, her face right up close to mine. I nod and put my mug down at my feet. The bending forward motion makes me feel like I'm going to be sick.

I stagger to the bathroom ignoring Edie's questions and sit on the floor, my head resting against the cold wall. Maybe this isn't just flu. I have a vague memory of watching some emergency medicine programme about meningitis. Is that

221

what this is? There's a trick I need to do, to find out . . . something to do with rolling a glass over me . . . Or could it be something else? Something even worse? Malaria? Typhoid fever? What are the symptoms of all these illnesses? Why don't I know?

I'm not sick, and eventually I drag myself out of the bathroom. Edie is waiting for me.

'Are you OK?' she asks for what must be the millionth time today.

I nod. 'I really have to go now.'

'No,' she says, moving towards the front door as if she's worried I'll make a run for it. 'You can't now. It's not safe.'

This seems like a weird choice of words but I can't really analyse it properly when I'm struggling just to stand upright.

Suddenly I feel very claustrophobic. The flat is too small. It feels damp and cramped. There's clutter everywhere. The heating is up too high. I need to get outside. I need fresh air in my lungs. I head for the door.

'Wait,' Edie says, moving towards the kitchen now. 'Look, I've made you a sandwich.' I look over and see there is indeed a neat little sandwich on a plate on the side, but I just shake my head.

'I can't, Edie. Sorry. I really have to go. I just need to be in my own bed.'

I put my hand on the door handle but as I do, I catch a flash of yellow out of the corner of my eye. I turn my head slightly and see that the door to the back room, Edie's spare room with the tiny en suite and little window strip, is open slightly. I've not seen inside that room since the day the agent showed us round. Edie's always said that she's using it to store junk, but it doesn't look like it's full of junk to me. In fact, it looks like she's spent quite some time doing it up, painting it this particularly vibrant shade of yellow.

Then, as I'm looking at the wall, squinting because the paint is so bright, I notice there's a photo on the wall. It's not in a frame, it's just stuck straight on the plaster with a drawing pin in each corner.

At first I think I'm imagining it, that my confused state is making me get things wrong, but when I take a step closer I realise I'm not mistaken. I do recognise the photo. It's the jumper that does it. The baby in the middle of the picture is wearing a rainbow striped jumper. My jumper.

The baby is me.

42

I push the door to the room open gently and stand in the doorway. I take a step towards the photo, my hand outstretched to touch it, as if that will help it make more sense.

It's definitely that photo. Definitely. It's the one I couldn't find, the one I thought Leon had taken. It's the photo of me and Mum and Dad on the wall at the beach, only someone's cut Mum out of the picture altogether, cut a whole slice of the photo away. It's just me and Dad now.

'Edie,' I call, my voice thick and shaky. 'Why have –'

Something hits me from behind, on my back. It's not a smack or a whack, more of a shove.

In my dozy state, I topple forward into the yellow room and fall onto my knees, onto a mattress that's been pushed against the wall and covered with a patchwork quilt.

Behind me, I hear the door shut and a key turn.

I clamber to my feet and turn around unsteadily. 'Edie? Edie!'

There's no reply. I go over to the door and try the handle but it's definitely locked. 'Edie!' I bang on the door with my palm. 'What the hell are you playing at?'

There's nothing for a few moments, no sounds of movement at all. Then I hear her voice. I can tell from the way it sounds that she has her face pushed up right into the gap at the edge.

'Anna,' she says, in this strange, calm tone. 'Anna, I want you to listen to me. Something's happened. Something we knew might happen but that we hoped wouldn't. It's Leon. He's done it. He's reported you. His video is everywhere. The police are looking for you. You cannot go out there. You need to stay here. I will keep you safe, I'll hide you. You don't need to worry. I won't let you go to prison but I need you to do as I say.'

I feel like I've been kicked in the stomach. It's happened. It's actually happened.

'When? How? What will . . . What's happening?' I can't formulate my questions. I can't work out what I want to ask. I just know I feel totally and completely confused.

'I found out when I went out to get your lemons. It's everywhere.'

'Lemons . . .' I repeat stupidly. Then I pull myself together enough to ask, 'What do you mean "everywhere"? What are people saying?'

'Just everywhere,' she repeats. 'They came here, looking for you when you were asleep. But I told them I hadn't seen you for days. I was good, Anna. I acted well.'

'Well . . . why didn't you tell me?'

'I didn't want to worry you, did I? I thought I could handle it. I've been slipping you the sleeping pills so you wouldn't try to leave but silly old Anna, you had to put a brave face on it, didn't you?' She chuckles then. It's a weird laugh, like

225

a naughty child. 'So now I've had to hide you away in here, haven't I? They won't find you in here. No, they won't.'

I try the door handle again even though I know it's no good. 'But why lock me in?'

No reply.

'Edie? Why have you locked the door? That makes no sense!'

I hear sounds of movement over in the lounge. I almost want to laugh, the whole situation seems so bizarre. I've always known Edie was a little eccentric but this seems plain weird. The way she's speaking, even the tone of her voice. I wonder if she's on drugs.

Then I think about what she said about sleeping pills. She's been drugging *me*? This whole time I've been feeling so awful is all because of pills? I'm pretty sure I haven't taken any actual, solid pills at any point so Edie must've been putting it in my food or drink. I remember the pie she made me yesterday and how I started to feel rough in the middle of eating it. This all feels very, very weird.

I step away from the door and stand in the middle of this strange, neon-yellow room.

Edie has adorned the walls with a range of posters and pictures – there's a montage of postcards from places all around the world – Bondi beach, Paris, Dubai, Goa. All places I want to go one day. All places I've more than likely told Edie I want to go one day. There's a movie poster advertising *Forrest Gump*. A film I like, a film that I told Edie was my favourite film, although now I come to think of it, I don't know if that's true.

There's a small chest of drawers next to the bed. In the top drawer, there are a few basics: deodorant, a toothbrush, toothpaste. In the two drawers below there are some clothes: a T-shirt, socks, pants. Brand new, labels still on. On top of the bedside table there's a book – a graphic novel that I told Edie is on my list to read, but is hard to get hold of. Where did she even find it?

On the floor at the end of the mattress there's a little CD player. I press the button to open the drawer and peer down at the CD to see if it's what I think it is. It is. It's *Various Positions* by Leonard Cohen, his first album to feature my favourite song, 'Hallelujah'.

I sit down on the mattress and rest the back of my head against the wall. This is all too surreal. I really do not know what is going on here. Edie has very carefully, very deliberately created a room just for me. She's been storing up these nuggets of information, secretly preparing everything. All the times she's claimed that I couldn't look in here, that it was too full of junk, she's been busily creating this. This weird little . . . cell. I don't know what to think. I had a feeling I'd become quite important to Edie but this is extreme.

I close my eyes for a second. I make myself breathe deeply. I need to compose myself. I need to be calm. Edie isn't mad, she's just unusual. She cares about me. That's why she's gone to all this trouble to create this room for me, to harbour me from the police. It wouldn't be what most people would do, but her intentions are good. She just wants to protect me. I can't come to harm while she wants to protect me.

Right?

But then I realise something, something about what Edie said.

She said she found out what Leon had done, that I was a wanted criminal, last night when she went out for the lemons. But she went out for the lemons *because* I felt rough, which means she'd *already* started drugging me. If, as she claims, she was giving me the pills to keep me here, to keep me hidden from the police, then how did she know to start giving them to me before she even knew I was in trouble?

This makes no sense. No sense at all.

43

'Edie,' I bang on the door. 'Edie, come here! What the hell are you playing at! Why are you doing this?'

I keep banging on the door, frantically at first but then I slow to a more rhythmic pounding. I keep it up for five, maybe ten minutes but I get no response at all. Eventually, I'm worn out and my palms are stinging. I sink down on the bed and rest my head on the pillow. I close my eyes. I need to think. I need to think this through rationally.

I snap my eyes back open when I hear a noise above me, a kind of scraping at the top of the wall. The little strip window that runs along the top of the room and out to the back garden slides open. I roll off the mattress and push myself to my feet. A plate with a sandwich on it and a mug of steaming tea is pushed through the space onto the window sill below. Then Edie's face appears in the gap. The strip is quite narrow – I can only properly see her eyes and the top of her nose when she's up close.

'You need to eat,' she says. 'And drink. You've been poorly, remember?'

'I haven't been poorly, Edie. You've been giving me pills.'

229

I keep my voice quite calm and neutral. I don't want it to sound like I'm accusing her. If what is happening here is that Edie is having some kind of mental episode, maybe a total breakdown, I don't want to do anything to push her over the edge. Although I reckon there's a pretty good chance that that ship has already sailed.

Edie frowns slightly and scrunches her nose up. 'Well, I had to. It was for your own good.'

I look at the sandwich and drink but I don't take them. Edie suddenly seems to clock why I might be reluctant to take her offerings.

'Oh, these aren't drugged, for heaven's sake! I only did it when I thought you were going to run off and land yourself in a lot of trouble. There's no need to keep giving you the stuff now, is there?'

No, I think, not now you've got me under lock and key.

Edie shakes her head and gives me an indulgent smile like I'm the one who's a bit mad. 'Silly old Anna.'

I take the plate and the cup and sip carefully at the tea. I decide I can just take it slow. If I start to feel woozy again, I'll ditch the stuff.

Edie turns to leave.

'Edie, wait!' I need to keep her here, keep her talking. I still don't know what's going on here. I don't know how much of what Edie has told me is true or how long she plans to keep me locked up, but I know the only way I'm going to get any answers is if I keep talking to her.

She turns back to the window, surprised. 'What is it? Would you like a biscuit?'

'No. No, thank you.' I need to decide what to say next. I need to be careful here. 'I love the room. I love all the pictures and posters and everything.'

'Oh, do you?' Edie smiles widely. 'Oh, I'm so pleased. I went to ever such a lot of trouble, you know. To make it perfect for you. Do you like the colour?'

I look around at the walls. I didn't even know you could get paint this dazzling. It's a pure, primary yellow. It reminds me of McDonalds. 'Uh, yeah. Sure. It's great. Very cheerful.'

'Yellow is your favourite. Remember?' She looks nervous again, anxious for approval.

Is it? If it ever was, I don't know if it is now. 'Yes, of course. My absolute favourite.'

Edie smiles again.

'Listen, Edie. I need to know exactly what's going on out there. What exactly has Leon done? What are people saying? Where did you hear about it?'

'It was when I went out for the lemons. That's when I found out.'

'Yes, I remember. But, I mean, *how*? Who told you?'

Edie squints off into the distance for a minute. Then she turns back to me and says, 'It was the man . . . in the shop. He says to me, "Have you seen Anna Roddick, because the police are looking for her?"'

I frown and run my hand through my hair. 'Which shop was it?'

Edie suddenly throws her hands up, exasperated. 'I don't know, do I? Just the shop in town where I got the lemons!'

'OK, OK,' I say, trying desperately to calm things. 'Sure.

Sorry. I just need to know what I'm dealing with.'

Edie pushes her face right up to the gap in the window. 'Anna, love. You don't need to worry. They can't find you here. You're safe now. Safe with me.'

I want to scream. I want to reach through the stupid little strip of a window and grab her and shake her and tell her she's being mental and she has to let me out. But I don't. Instead, I smile and say, 'I know. I really appreciate it.'

Edie slides the window shut and disappears. This time I let her go. I need some time to think properly. I need to think of a new strategy, a plan for when I next speak to her.

The one big relief is that I'm now pretty sure that Edie's story about Leon reporting me is a massive lie. Her timings don't add up at all and, what's more, the idea of some random shop worker happening to mention me by name sounds totally bizarre. There's a chance, I suppose, that Leon has grassed me up, and that Edie has just got herself in a muddle about how she found out about it, but I think it's more likely that the whole thing is one big concoction of lies.

This, at least, is good. It definitely means less to worry about when I do make it out of here. But the problem of how exactly I am going to make it out still remains.

About half an hour after Edie delivered my sandwich and tea, I've finished both and don't feel too ill at all. I think the drugs from before are wearing off and I feel pretty sure that she hasn't added anything new to my latest meal.

I stand up and go over to the door. I knock three times. 'Edie! Are you there?' I'm careful not to sound too aggressive or angry. I'm just calling her over. I want a chat.

At first I think she's going to ignore me – or that she's gone out – but then I hear the little window slat slide open again.

'Did you call, love? Do you want something?'

'I was just thinking about what you said, about everything that's going on out there. I'd really like to see for myself.'

'Anna, you don't need –'

'I *know* I . . .' I breathe. Stay calm, Anna. 'I know I don't need to worry about it, but I'm just . . . interested. I just want to check the news online. Would you mind bringing me my phone?'

Edie's eyes are wide suddenly. 'No! Of course you can't use your phone! They'll trace you straight away through that thing. They'll be knocking down the door in five seconds flat and hauling you off to court!'

I close my eyes for a second. I suddenly feel like I'm going to cry. How have things ended up like this? How am I here?

'They won't. Not if I just go on the internet. They can't trace that. I won't make any calls.'

Edie suddenly lets out a loud, exasperated sigh. 'Anna, I said *no*! Come on, love. Don't be like this. I'm trying here, you know? You've done some very silly things and silly things have consequences. I'm trying my absolute best to do what's right for you but you can't keep fighting me. I'm getting cross with you now so I'm going to go because I don't like it when we have words, but I'll bring you your tea later.'

Before I can say anything else, she's snapped the window shut and I'm alone again.

I do cry now. I sink down onto my mattress, bury my face in my knees to hide my eyes from that oppressive flaring yellow and I cry until my head aches. I wonder if Edie will come and check on me but either she doesn't hear me or she doesn't want to acknowledge how her behaviour is making me feel.

When there are no more tears left in me, I stretch out on the mattress and look at the ceiling. It's only then that I properly think about what my dad said about her in that voicemail. Edie Southwood is a lunatic. I realise then that she must've been lying the whole time. About everything. She was never tricked. No one told her Dad was dead. She made it up. She's been lying to me since the day we met. She's been a lunatic the whole time I've known her.

She just hid it better before.

44

Eventually I fall asleep. I guess I still have some sleeping pills left in my system because I sleep soundly, without any dreams, without stirring at all. It's the sound of the window scraping open that wakes me.

Edie slides a glass of orange juice and a plate of poached eggs on toast onto the window sill. Bloody poached eggs. If I ever get out of this, you can be pretty certain that I won't be having poached eggs for a very long time.

'Hello, sleepyhead!' comes Edie's cheery voice. 'How are you this morning?'

'OK, but . . . I'd like to get up really. Have a bath, maybe watch some telly with you? I'm sure they wouldn't find me if I was just in the lounge with you. I'd still be safe.'

She's quiet for a long time. I wonder if she's wandered off, lost interest in me. Then suddenly her face appears at the window.

'You know, Anna, my love, I'm going to tell you a little story.'

She adjusts her position slightly, so she's leaning on the window sill. I look up at her, to show I'm listening. I need to keep her engaged.

'When I was eight, I was supposed to be taking part in a swimming gala. Just a silly local one, you know, just for little kids. But my word, was I excited about it! I spent weeks practising my backstroke, making my dad take me to the pool every weekend, running up and down the stairs to work on my stamina. Then the day of the gala came. I woke up early, of course, excited, butterflies in my tummy. Until I try to sit up and I'm sick all down my front and I realise it's not butterflies at all!' She laughs at the memory. 'I was sick, Anna. Really ill. So of course, Dad says, well you can't go swimming today. And I was horrified: no, Dad I said, I'm fine, I'm well enough. I won't be sick again, I promise! And Dad wasn't sure but he didn't like to disappoint me, so he said we'd see how I was at lunchtime.'

'So . . . did you get to go?' I'm not sure where this story is going but it's definitely better to keep her here, talking, where I can reason with her, rather than on the other side of the flat.

'Well, I was sick three more times that morning. I felt awful, that was the truth of the situation. But when Dad asked me, I lied and said I hadn't been sick. Said I felt fine, raring to go. And he still wasn't sure, but in the end he let me have my way. He always did, my old dad. So I'm standing at the side of the pool, ready to dive in, ready to show them what I'm made of, and I realise it's coming. But it all happens too quick for me to move. So I'm just sick again, right there over the edge of the pool into the water. And the whole audience makes this groaning noise, and all the other little kids on the edge back away and I'm just stood there looking down at the sick in the pool and feeling the worst I have ever felt in my

236

life until my dad runs on down from the stands and scoops me up and carries me into the changing rooms. The whole gala has to be cancelled so they can clean the pool and these boys at school start calling me Sickface Southwood and the name stuck for years. So even now, I think, I wish I'd listened to my dad.'

She stops talking and I guess that's the end of the story.

'He was good, my dad. A good man.' Then she adds quietly, 'He's dead now.'

'I know. I'm sorry,' I say. 'But . . .'

I'm not sure how to phrase the question. I want to ask what her point is. I want to ask what the hell her puking in a swimming pool as a kid has got to do with her keeping me locked up now, thirty years later. Maybe this is her explanation for why she's such a loon? The whole Sickface Southwood thing has damaged her.

Suddenly she starts up again. 'So, you see what I mean, my love. I know sometimes we want to do things but sometimes we can't. We have to stay put and do as we're told. Parents know best. We just want to look after you.'

Then all of a sudden, she slides the window shut and I'm left alone again to think about whether I should be more freaked out by the fact that Edie genuinely thinks she's doing me good or that she's just referred to herself as my parent.

I wonder if Edie will go to work today. I can't hear any sounds out there, no telly or radio or running taps – maybe she's gone already? I start to feel a tightness in my chest at the thought of being alone. It seems strange, I know, that I should want Edie nearby, but the fact of the matter is, it's better that she's there than isn't there. What if there's a fire? What if she just doesn't come back? If she has an accident or just decides not to bother coming back to this flat, to this life? To start a new life, somewhere else in the country, with some poor new sucker as her victim? What will happen to me then? Will anyone ever find me?

I wonder if this is my fate. To be locked up like this. Maybe, since I pushed Shay, being locked away and punished has been embedded in my destiny.

There was this film that George made us watch once, where all these kids missed a flight and then the plane crashed, so they thought they'd all cheated death. But then later, in the rest of the film, death catches up with them one by one and kills them in other ways instead. It was their fate; there was no escaping it. Maybe that is like this. I've managed to avoid being locked up for a while by keeping my crime a secret but now my destiny has caught up with me.

I sit down on the mattress and make myself breathe slowly. Come on, Anna. Don't lose it. I realise that if Edie has gone to work, all I can do is distract myself and hope the time passes as quickly as possible. I listen to my Leonard Cohen CD twice through. I cut my fingernails with the clippers Edie has provided for me in my bedside drawer. I read the whole graphic novel. Then I get into the bed and hide my face in the covers and imagine I'm anywhere but here.

I guess eventually I fall asleep because once again the sound of the window opening wakes me up. It's dark outside now.

'Hey there, stranger!' comes Edie's voice. 'Did you miss me? I brought you a present home from work.'

A paper bag appears on the window sill. I recognise the print. It's from the shop. A bag of fudge. I know I should stand up. I should take the fudge, be suitably grateful and try to engage Edie in a line of conversation that might somehow, at some point, persuade her to let me out. But I just can't face it. I just can't be bothered. I can't get it in me to even push myself upright. I just stay there, lying completely still on the mattress.

'Anna? You OK, love?'

I don't move.

'Anna?'

When she says my name for the second time, her voice sounds anxious. And that shift in tone is what gives me my idea.

A plan that I think might just get me out of here.

45

'Anna, love? Are you asleep?'

I don't reply. I'm not going to reply. Because what I've just realised is that Edie doesn't actually wish me harm.

All this – this carefully designed room, all the food, keeping me here at all – this is how Edie thinks she can show she cares for me. This is Edie's way of looking after me. She's keeping me in this room because she's scared I'll leave. The only way I can beat that fear is to trump it with an even bigger one. And I have a pretty good idea that the one thing that would freak Edie out more than if I left her for ever is if I was dead.

Or at least ill enough that there's a very real danger I could kick the bucket unless she steps in to sort it out.

This means that the best plan for me right now isn't to start a conversation. There's nothing I can say to talk myself out of this. The best plan now is for me to say nothing at all.

I close my eyes and I try to angle my limbs so I look slightly uncomfortable. If she looks through the window I need to look unnaturally unconscious, as opposed to just dozing.

'Anna?' she says again.

There's a pause. I let myself hope that she's already making her way through the side door to the building and back into the flat to come and open the door to check on me. But then I hear a chuckle. 'Sleepyhead. You get your rest, my love.' Then she slides the window shut and I'm alone again.

The disappointment is like a punch in the stomach, but I deal with it by telling myself that this doesn't matter. It delays things, but the plan is still solid. I just need to persevere.

I won't take the bag of fudge down. I won't make any more noise – no trips to the loo, no Leonard Cohen, nothing. She'll be back. I'll repeat the performance. At some point she'll have to twig that I'm not just napping.

It's probably an hour later when she returns. She notices the untouched paper bag as soon as she opens the window.

'Anna? Didn't you want your fudge, love? It's rum and raisin, your favourite?'

I'm silent. I shifted back into my unnaturally unconscious position as soon as I heard the window opening.

'Anna, are you OK?'

There's the sound of scrambling around. I guess she's looking for something to stand on so she can get a proper look through the window. She's going to look at me. My pose is finally going to get a viewing.

'Anna? Oh god, Anna!' Her voice is louder. I can't open my eyes but I know she's looking at me. 'Anna!'

I hear the sound of her footsteps. She's running away from the window and back to the house. I smile to myself.

I hear the key turning in the lock and my impulse is to climb up, to make a dash for it, to bulldoze my way past Edie and

241

make my bid for freedom. But I force myself to stay in position. If she gets wind of the fact I'm faking too early she'll block my path. She's bigger than me and she's already shown once that she can shove me into this room and hold me here. And if I mess this up and give myself away this whole scheme will be ruined for ever. It's definitely not something that would work a second time.

I stay still. Edie enters.

She rushes over to me. 'Anna, oh, Anna, what's happening to you?' She puts her hand on my forehead, then she shakes my shoulders.

I make sure I stay completely limp. I don't let any signs of life slip out at all. She puts her face near mine, I can sense how close she is, smell her perfume, but I can't open my eyes. I figure she's seeing if I'm breathing. I hold my breath. I hope she doesn't stay there long.

'Oh no, oh no, oh no.' She puts one arm under my legs and another around my neck.

She's going to try to lift me. I don't think she'll be able to, but that doesn't matter. This will be a good opportunity. This is where I'll overcome her when she's off balance. I'll topple her, and I'll make a break for it. This is it. I'm ready.

Suddenly, there's a noise from the hallway. Three sharp knocks and a shout. 'Edie! Edie, are you in there?' Then another three knocks.

Edie freezes. 'James?' she says in a hushed voice.

I feel my heartbeat quicken. James? Dead/not-dead-dad James? Could that really be my father out there? I don't know his voice well enough but Edie surely must do. Although she

242

could be deluded, assuming every man she hears is James, come to claim her back. And I don't know if I really care at this point. Anyone will do.

'Not *now*, James,' Edie says, in the same hushed tone. She's whispering. There's no way he could hear her out there, but I don't think he's supposed to. She's talking to herself.

He bangs on the front door again. 'Edie! I just want to talk to you. See if we can work things out.'

Are you serious? I think. You can't seriously want to 'work things out'? I don't know exactly what the hell has gone on between you two nutters but either you pretended to be dead or, as seems more likely given recent developments, Edie pretended you were dead. This is surely not the behaviour of normal people in a healthy relationship. I don't think these are the kinds of things that can really be worked out with a nice meal out and a promise to spend more quality time together. But none of that matters to me, not now. I need to make a decision and I need to make it quickly because making the wrong one could prove disastrous.

Do I continue my plan, lie completely still, hope James disappears and let Edie continue her rescue mission? Or do I call out, and hope James hears me and busts through the front door to help spring me out of here?

Think, Anna. *Think*.

I decide to stay quiet. I'm on the brink of escape. If I shout out now I'll only scare Edie and then who knows what she'll do. She might have a weapon on her, a knife. She might push it to my throat and use me as some weird bargaining tool in her negotiations with her ex. I can do without that, thank you very much.

There's one more knock on the door, then I hear James shout, 'Fine, if that's how you want to play it.'

I hear a woman's voice then, although I can't make out what she says. I hear James mutter something in reply. He sounds irritated. I guess this must be his new girlfriend, the one I heard in the background when I spoke to him on the phone. Then I hear footsteps walking quickly down the corridor, down the side of the flat and away. I feel myself deflate. Have I just let my first contact with the outside, my only shot at rescue walk away?

'James! Dad! Anyone! Help!'

I don't know where it came from. I didn't mean to do it. It wasn't in the plan. It just came out from the panic. It just burst right out of me. Edie spins around. I push myself up and try to get off the mattress so I can make a run for it before she realises what's going on.

'Anna!' She looks shocked.

'You have to let me go!' I charge at her. I'm going to push her out the way. I can do this.

She's too quick for me. One quick shove and I'm on my back on the mattress again. Then she slips out of the door. I hear the key turn in the lock.

'No!' I shout. 'NO!'

I push my fists into my eyes and I cry tears of pure frustration. I am so angry with myself. I was so close and I let my panic take over and ruin everything. Why do you have to be such an absolute moron, Anna?

I wonder if Edie will reappear at the window, to tell me off for scaring her, to give me another speech about what is and isn't for my own good. But she doesn't. She doesn't come anywhere near the yellow room. I suppose I'm being punished.

I lie flat on my back, looking at the ceiling. I count to nine hundred and ninety nine, then I stop and start again from one. I do this four times. Then I just lie there not moving at all.

My mind feels completely blank. Numb. I wonder if this is what meditation is like. I don't know how much time passes. It could be ten minutes. It could be ten hours.

'Edith!' The shout is loud, insistent. It takes me a minute to work out where it's coming from. 'Edith Southwood, open the door, please.'

There's no reply. I sit up on my mattress, listening hard. What's going on here?

'Edith Southwood, this is the police. Please open the door.'

There's still no sound from inside the flat. I don't even know if Edie's still here. Maybe she's gone out. I'm on my feet. I'm over by the door. I bang on it over and over with my fists. 'Help me! I'm in here! Please, someone, help me!'

There's another voice. This time it's from behind me. It's from the window. Someone outside my window.

'Anna? Is that you? Oh god, Anna!'

'Mum!' I run over to the window and stand on my mattress. The window slides open. I see a hand. I reach up and take it. 'Mum!'

There is a huge crash, cracking wood. There are stomping footsteps. There are voices – two men. 'Anna? Anna?'

The door is unlocked. A policeman stands in the doorway. 'Anna Roddick? Are you OK? Are you injured?'

Before I can answer, the policeman is shoved aside and Mum crashes into the room. 'Anna!'

She steps forward, she touches my cheek with her hand, she pulls me into a hug. I just hang there, limp. I'm exhausted.

I hear a voice outside. 'Oh god, oh Christ!'

The policeman dashes out to the lounge. Mum and I follow and when we do, I see my father for the first time in ten years.

He looks the same, I suppose. Just older and thinner, like his photo from his work's website.

He's on his knees and he's leaning over Edie, who's lying on the sofa completely motionless, her arm hanging limp. She is doing a good unnaturally unconscious pose. It certainly gives mine a run for its money but then I have a feeling that hers isn't fake. There's an empty pill bottle on the floor by her side.

My father turns to look at us.

'She's gone and done it this time. She's killed herself, the bloody fool.'

46

It's been three months since Edie tried to kill herself.

She didn't succeed, although by all accounts she would have if it hadn't been for my mother, my father and PC Heyward arriving when they did. She took a massive overdose of triazolam, the same sleeping pill she'd used to keep me dozy that first night. It was only a few days after I escaped the yellow room that I really considered what it would've meant if her attempt had worked: my one connection to the outside world, my connection to food, to escape, could've been lying dead and probably undiscovered for quite some time.

Edie was taken to a hospital to get the drugs out of her system, and then onto some kind of mental health place, somewhere she could have therapy and counselling, that kind of thing.

The Crown Prosecution Service decided it 'wasn't in the public interest' to prosecute her for locking me up. The kindly policeman explained this to me gently, as if I was expected to object, but the truth was, seeing Edie dragged through some drawn-out court process was the last thing I wanted. I didn't really fancy putting myself through it either, for that matter.

I had to talk to the various policemen and women for a bit and some social worker types too. I told them all about how I met Edie and what had happened over the last few days. I didn't tell them about the sleeping pills in my dinner bit though. I decided there was no need. I don't know if it was the relief at being out of that room or the fact that Edie was lying at death's door, but I didn't really feel angry at all. I just felt sad.

Dad came home with me and Mum. I found that surprising, although I suppose it would've been weirder if he'd just driven straight back up to London without talking to us at all.

We sat in the lounge, Mum next to me, holding my hand, Dad on the sofa opposite. It was strange for us, the hand-holding. But it was nice too, really. When I'd first been released from the room, Mum had hugged me and I realised that it had been so long since she'd done that that we felt all different, up close together. I was the same height as her now. The last time she held me close like that I'd fitted under her chin easily.

We all had tea. Mum kept asking me what I wanted, what I needed, but Edie had kept me quite well fed so I didn't really need anything. In the end Mum settled on tea because that's what people do.

Mum explained that when I'd been missing for a day she called Sienna and grilled her on where I could be. Although I hadn't mentioned Edie for a long time, both Sienna and George got the feeling I was still seeing her, so they gave Mum a brief overview of who she was and how I knew her. Mum had immediately been suspicious about the whole death aspect to the situation and it hadn't taken her long on the phone to work out it was indeed a load of rubbish. She immediately summoned Dad down here to sort out the 'unhinged girlfriend who's kidnapped our daughter'.

Mum and Dad were both there, that first time when James had called around. The woman in the background I'd heard him speaking to wasn't some new girlfriend: it was Mum. She was the one who decided to come back with the police.

Dad talked a lot as we sat there in the lounge – mostly about how mad Edie was and how he'd always had 'this kind of behaviour' from her. It annoyed me. It reminded me of how he was on the phone that time, huffing and puffing and sighing with all the tedious inconvenience of it all.

After a while he said, 'The one good thing about all this is that it's given us a chance to get back in touch. Don't you think, Anna?'

Next to me Mum made a very quiet 'hmph' noise but she didn't say anything. I looked at my father over my cup of tea. 'But you could've got in touch before, if you'd wanted to. You knew where I was. We've always lived here.'

Dad looked uncomfortable, shifting in his seat. He uncrossed and recrossed his legs. 'Well, yes, of course, but sometimes it takes circumstances to conspire to . . . I mean, we're all busy people and these things can be . . .'

Mum stepped in. 'Five minutes of playing the knight in shining armour doesn't really make up for the last ten years, James.'

Anyone else might've sounded bitter then, but not Mum. She delivered this line in the same way she says everything else – perfectly cool and calm. I liked it.

249

Dad sighed and put his mug down at his feet. Then he stood up and reached for his coat from the arm of the sofa. 'Fine. Well, if that's how you feel, maybe I should just go.'

I don't know if he expected us to stop him at this point, but neither of us said anything. I just took a sip of my tea and kept watching him. This seemed to irritate him.

'I see you've brought her up to be just like you,' he said to Mum. 'A cold bitch.'

I felt myself flinch then. I hadn't expected that. If I'd had any last glimmer of interest in getting to know him left in me, it evaporated then.

Mum squeezed my hand a little tighter. 'Don't call our daughter a bitch, please, James,' she said, still composed as anything. I almost wanted to laugh.

Dad fiddled around trying to zip up his coat, getting it all wrong on account of his rage. 'I honestly don't know what you women want from me. It's like nothing is ever enough. You just take and take and take, you wring a man out, leave him like a used dishcloth.'

Mum didn't say anything, so neither did I. We just kept looking at him. Then he'd had enough. He stormed out of the room, slammed the front door and sped off in his flashy open-top car.

'Sorry about your father,' Mum said, still cool but now with a tiny twinkle in her eye.

I hugged her. She seemed surprised, but she hugged me back. We stayed like that for a long time.

'Maybe it would be better if he *was* dead,' I said eventually.

Mum pulled away then and looked at me, frowning slightly.

'Sorry,' I said quickly. Maybe that was too harsh, even for Mum. I was anxious to avoid anything that might lead to a row. 'It's just, I thought he was dead, and then not dead and . . .'

Mum sat down on the sofa and gently pulled me down next to her.

'Tell me everything that happened. Right from the first letter that woman sent you.'

So I did, and Mum listened, taking sips of her tea, but not saying anything, not reacting at all.

When I finished, she sighed. 'Well, for what it's worth, I'm sorry. I'm sorry you couldn't tell me about the letter, about the phone calls, about Edie. It's my fault, I know.'

I wasn't sure how best to respond to that. Had it been her fault? I probably hadn't helped. I didn't know. In the end, we said nothing for a while, and then I asked her about what had happened when I was born, about her mother being ill. I wanted to know if what Edie had told me was true. I didn't see how it could be. The idea of a baby keeping someone with cancer alive was just so random, so illogical – I just couldn't see a person like Mum believing in a plan like that.

Mum looked down at her hands. She looked sad. Then she ran her hands through her hair and said, 'The mind can have a profound influence on physical well-being. It's been proven many times. Hope, in certain situations, can have a marked impact.'

So it was true.

I *had* been planned, but I had failed to uphold my part of the plan. Mum's mum had died. The thought of me hadn't been enough to keep her alive.

I wanted to cry suddenly, but I didn't because Mum had never been good with crying and I didn't want to spoil things. Neither of us said anything for a while.

'We'll try harder, we'll be better,' Mum said eventually. 'Both of us.'

I just nodded.

And things between us have been better since that day. I'm not going to say they've completely transformed – we're not the best of mother/daughter friends, going on shopping trips together and doing karaoke – but she's been making an effort, I can tell.

She always comes out of her study when I get home from school. She tries to cook for me two or three days a week. I try to do my part by being polite, showing an interest in her work. I ask her advice on things that I know will please her, things that will keep her inside her comfort zone – science homework, mostly. The other day I told her I'm thinking about doing biology A-level and she looked about as delighted as I've ever seen her.

When Dad was sitting there on the sofa that day, droning on about the mad women he has to put up with, it suddenly occurred to me who he reminded me of. He reminded me of Leon. Smug, superior Leon. I'll tell you the best part of this whole situation: I haven't seen Leon since it all happened because as we speak he is nine thousand miles away. That weird text I got from Sienna the morning after my sleeping-pill induced stupor was right: Leon has gone to live in South Africa. I thought it was all just a wonderful stroke of luck until two days after I got home, when I got a visit from Leon's mum, from R.M. Jakes-Field herself.

I felt a bit star struck seeing her there on the door-step. I didn't think she'd have that effect on me – I thought I'd only ever be able to see her as mother and creator of the abominable Leon, no matter how many millions she's made from writing stories – but I'd never seen her in real life before, only ever on the TV or on big billboard posters so it made me feel funny, seeing her outside my front door, in a smart woollen coat, carrying a neat black handbag.

'Oh,' I said when I saw her. 'Hello.'

'Anna? I'm Rebecca Jakes-Field. Leon's mother.'

'Uh . . . yes. I know.'

'May I come in?'

We sat at the kitchen table and she explained that the night Edie had gone out to find my lemons, she'd accosted Rebecca as she was getting into her car.

'She was perfectly calm and reasonable,' Rebecca explained. 'She told me exactly what had happened when you were looking after Shay Bradstock next door and more importantly, how Leon had been treating you since.'

I wasn't sure what to say to this. I still wasn't sure why Rebecca was here. She didn't seem to be angry with me, but I wondered if she wanted to get my side of the story, if she was imagining that I would contradict Edie's version and tell her that her wonderful Leon had been nothing but the perfect gentleman.

'I spoke to Leon about it straight away, of course. He tried to laugh it off, pretend that you had exaggerated things, but

I know my son. This isn't the first time he's treated a girl like this. I'm so sorry, Anna, that he behaved in that way. He's spoilt, I'm afraid to say. If he can't have what he wants then he'll scheme and manipulate and bully until he gets it. It's not his fault entirely. It hasn't been good for him, me being . . . well, my career being so public. So for his own good – but more importantly for everyone else's – I've sent him to South Africa to have a long hard think about his behaviour.'

'To Africa?' This seemed extreme to me, no matter what Leon had done. Can you just send a person to Africa against their will? Maybe it was just because the family was well-off – this is the rich-family version of being sent to your room.

Rebecca laughed then. 'Oh, don't look so horrified. My husband's brother – Leon's uncle – has a maize farm just outside Johannesburg. He'll have food and shelter, but he'll have to work a lot harder than he's used to. I can tell you one thing for certain, and that's that good old Uncle Carl won't let him shirk his duties so he can work on his writing. They live a rural lifestyle where they're interested in how hard you work the land and how well you can hunt. They're not interested in me or my silly made-up stories over there and they won't be interested in Leon's either. It'll be character-building for him.'

I nodded but I didn't say anything. It was a relief to know he was so far away but, the truth was, Leon wasn't my only concern. 'But the boy . . . Shay . . .? And his dad?'

'Oh god, of course, that was the main thing I came to say!' Rebecca said. She shook her head and laughed at her own absent-mindedness. 'I spoke to Gerrard myself. I told him what had happened. He was hardly bothered at all. A child like Shay is often getting into scrapes and I daresay Gerrard has given him a whack himself from time to time. I saw that nasty video Leon had created and made him delete it. I know what he told you about assault and bodily harm and all that nonsense so I can see how you were nervous, but I can assure you the police won't be paying you a visit any time soon. I don't really think the police spend their days investigating every little playground bump and scrape!'

I felt myself flush a little then. I'd been an idiot, hadn't I? I've been exactly as Leon had wanted me to be. He acted confident, so although I hated him, I believed him. I believed that he knew more than me. And there I'd been, thinking Edie was the naive one in all this.

Rebecca apologised again for Leon and I said it was OK, because there wasn't really anything else to say.

When she was gone I kept going over and over how stupid I'd been to believe Leon, to let him do that to me. In the end I had to tell myself to just take the positive from the situation: Shay was OK. Gerrard was fine. I wasn't going to spend the rest of my life on the run from the law, from the press. From karma.

47

Six months to the day since I got that first letter from Edie, I got another one from her. I recognised the handwriting at once.

I took the envelope upstairs, shut my bedroom door and sat on my bed.

Dear Anna,

I don't know if you will even read this letter. Maybe you'll see my name at the end and tear it up straight away. Or maybe you won't open it at all. I hope you do open it, though. There's so much I want to say to you.

Firstly, and most obviously I suppose, I'm sorry. I'm sorry for going totally bonkers-in-the-head and locking you up like a hamster. I know sorry doesn't really even begin to cut it, but like I say, I was bonkers-in-the-head. Thing is, Anna, I knew it was bonkers, even when I was doing it. I just got desperate and scared and it made me act like a nutcase.

I supposed you've realised by now that I knew James wasn't dead. I know I was wrong to say that he was. And to carry on saying he was, even when you'd spoken to him! I just didn't know what else to do. The lie had got too much. I couldn't see a way out.

You should know that I did think it once, though. I did think he was dead, for a while. He let me think it. It was some sick little joke he came up with with his friend. That Marcus – remember him? Or maybe it was more than a joke. Maybe it was meant to be his escape plan. Anyway, that was when I wrote to you. I told you before I realised. Before I knew it was a lie.

It turned out to be a hard joke for him to keep going though – pretending to not exist – because I found out the truth soon enough. But by that time, you'd agreed to see me and I didn't want to say anything that would change your mind. I still wanted to meet you, you see. So badly.

I was just curious at first, Anna. I just wanted to see what you were like. You were my connection to him. Alive or dead, James was still out of my life and you were about as close as I was going to get to him. I knew you existed, but not much else. He would never talk about you, you see. Said it was all in the past. And then I met you and it was so interesting for me – you looked like James, had some of his mannerisms,

*and that was fascinating. After our first meeting, I
just wanted to know more about you. I started coming
down to the coast – every day, almost. Sometimes I'd
see you with your friends or on your way to school.
I don't know what I was hoping to see. I don't know
how I thought it would help. All I can tell you, by way
of comparison, is that once your dad told me he liked
Stanley Kubrick films and the next time he finished
with me (there were hundreds of times) I went out and
hired every single Stanley Kubrick film I could get my
hands on. I watched them all, studying every detail.
I don't even know why. Coming down, following you
around – it was like that. Desperately clinging on to
any connection. I know, I know. Bonkers.*

*And then you saw me, of course, hiding on the pier like
a right fruitcake. You should've run a mile then, Anna!
But I'm glad you didn't because you were so lovely to
me, helping me with my CV and listening to me prattle
on. I just liked you, Anna. That's the honest truth of it.
And the longer it went on – the lie – the harder it was
to end it. I just didn't want to ruin things.*

*I guess it was obvious to you really but I wasn't
friends with anyone in that band. I don't have any
friends at all, of course! It wasn't a friend's gig. No.
I just wanted to come and see you, to take you out.
It's hard to explain, Anna, but when you don't have
anything in your life, when it all feels so full of cold,*

empty pain, it's quite easy to get attached to the good people, to the only people who don't make you feel like a total lunatic.

I used to tell you how I always wanted a family. Once James had washed his hands of me, you were the closest thing I had. When you'd tell me about your problems – with Leon, with your mum – I felt like I could actually help you. I'd always imagined myself being a mum to little kids, singing nursery rhymes, pushing them on the swings, but I'd never realised how much I wanted someone to talk to me, to ask my advice.

I started to think how lovely it would be if you came to live with me. I felt like your mum didn't deserve you, didn't deserve to be a mum, and that I would do it better. I felt like I had the right to have you with me. So I started to do that little room up for you. I got carried away, I suppose, buying all the bits and pieces, decorating it yellow for you. I just thought that if I made it so lovely, so perfect for you, you wouldn't be able to refuse.

But then when it was all done, I got nervous. I got scared you'd reject me. That's when I did that totally bonkers – totally wrong – thing and put the sleeping pills in your dinner. I knew that was bad. I knew, I knew, I knew. I just thought if you were a bit dozy you'd want to stay over and then I'd look after you

*and you'd want to stay longer and then . . . I don't
even know. I thought maybe you'd end up living with
me by accident.*

*That night when you were conked out on the sofa
I went to talk to Leon's mother. That Rebecca, the
author. It just came to me, the idea, that day in the
lounge. It wasn't even planned. I just thought, If only
that boy's mother knew what he was like . . . And
then I thought, that's it, this is perfect! I'd seen her on
the telly and she always seemed like a bit of a tough
cookie to me – you know, a no-nonsense type. I thought,
maybe if she knew she'd put a stop to it all. But then
when I went up to her, when I explained it all, she was
so cold. She didn't say anything at all. Not a word, the
whole time I was talking. And when I finished she just
said, 'Thank you for bringing it to my attention,' and
walked off into the night.*

*And then I was scared, Anna, I can tell you! What
have I done, I thought. Rebecca is going to go straight to
Leon and tell him what I've said and then everything
is going to be a thousand times worse for you. I didn't
know what Leon might do to you then. So that's when
I knew I had to keep you with me. Whatever it took, I
had to keep you safe with me. I wouldn't let him near
you. I knew I couldn't keep you there for ever. I thought
I'd have a better idea eventually, that I'd be able to
sort it out. I just needed time . . .*

*Anyway, Anna, I hope you're well. I sincerely hope
that things with Leon have improved. I still think
you should just tell the Bradstock boy's father. I think
whatever happens it'll be better that being wrapped
around Leon's little finger for the rest of your life.
Maybe tell your mum? I think maybe if you gave her
a chance, maybe she'd be better than you think.
I don't know.*

*I'm living in this little place in the country now. It's
a 'retreat' – that's what they call it. It's where you
go when you're not totally bonkers-in-the-head any
more but when you're not quite trusted to be left
to your own devices. And I'll tell you something,
Anna – I quite like it here. I've got my own little flat,
the gardens are lovely and there are lots of other
people around to chat to. All bonkers too, of course, but
beggars can't be choosers. And maybe it's nice not to
have everyone looking at me funny for a change.*

*I'm better now, Anna, I am. I'm sure you probably
don't care one way or the other but I'm glad I didn't
see myself off with those pills. I didn't want that. Not
really. I just thought I was out of options, you know?*

*I hope you've got to the bottom of this letter, Anna. I
really think you're such a wonderful girl, whatever
you think of me. I would've been proud if you were my
daughter, honestly I would. My address is at the top*

*and I hope you'll consider writing to me one day. It
would be lovely to hear your news. And of course, I'm
allowed visitors too, if you speak to reception . . . but,
I know. I can hardly expect that after everything.*

*Sorry again, Anna. So sorry for everything I put you
through. And if we never speak again, best of luck for
the future, my love. You deserve a good one.*

Love,
Edie x

I put the letter back in the envelope and tuck it in the drawer
next to my bed.

I feel if anyone knew she'd asked me to go and see her, they'd
be falling over themselves to warn me off. I suppose they'd be
right. So why do I have this feeling like going to see her, going
to talk to her, is something I really, really want to do?

I think it's because things were cut off so abruptly. For
those few short months, Edie was my best friend. I would
never have called her that to anyone – especially not George
and Sienna – but that fact is, she was the only one who knew
about my problems and the only person I really trusted. And
then suddenly she was gone.

I wanted to talk to her about it – about what she'd done, and
what was and wasn't the truth, about everything – but no one
thought of that. They just assumed I was scared of her, that
she must've traumatised me in some way and that I should be
encouraged to forget her.

That feeling hasn't gone away. I still want to talk to her. At the very least, I want to thank her for sorting out Leon. She did brilliantly there.

To give George and Sienna credit where it's due, they've actually been quite good about everything that happened. There was never a word of 'told you so'. In fact, they apologised for slagging Edie off and said they felt like they'd made the problem worse by forcing me to see Edie in secret. But despite all that, I still have a pretty good idea what they'll make of this letter. No way, they'll say. It's over now. Don't stir things up again. Sienna will give me a dramatic wide-eyed look. George will make a joke.

What I really need is some reasoned, detached advice without any melodrama. And I know just the person to give it.

When I pass Mum the letter she reads it over without saying anything. Her face is impassive. She doesn't seem alarmed or angry – even at the bits about her. She just asks me what I think. Then quite coolly and calmly, she tells me what she thinks. We discuss a few options, and we decide what to do.

I go downstairs and I dial the number at the bottom of Edie's letter.

'Hello, I'd like to arrange to visit Edith Southwood, please.'

'Certainly, I can put that in the book for you. Just one visitor pass?'

'No, two please. One for me, one for my mother.'

Acknowledgements

Thank you to my agent, Jo Williamson, for a great couple of years. I hope there are many more.

Of course, huge thanks to everyone at Hot Key Books, but especially Emma Matthewson, Jenny Jacoby (who could forget Jenny Jacoby? Not me, that's for sure), and the indefatigable Rosi Crawley and Jen Green.

Thank you to all of the book bloggers for their incredible enthusiasm, but Jim Dean deserves a special mention.

I've been lucky enough to make a whole range of new author friends in the last couple of years who have helped me in lots of ways, but I'd especially like to thank Abie Longstaff for the sage industry advice, Sarah Crossan for some fairly invaluable support, and Lisa Williamson for a bit of both, plus lots of fun.

Thanks to Mum and Dad, of course, and to Lottie, who didn't actually do anything but got in a mood when I missed her out last time.

Biggest thanks, as always and for everything, to Amber.

Jess Vallance

Jess Vallance works as a freelance writer specialising in educational materials and has written articles on everything from business accounting to embalming a body. Jess lives in Brighton. Her first novel for Hot Key Books was *Birdy*.

Follow Jess at www.jessvallance.com or on Twitter: @JessVallance1

HOT KEY BOOKS

Thank you for choosing a Hot Key book.

If you want to know more about our authors and what we publish, you can find us online.

You can start at our website

www.hotkeybooks.com

And you can also find us on:

We hope to see you soon!